Wrong Earful . . .

The phone rang again. Furious, Carol grabbed up the receiver: "After what you've done, Jerry Powers, I'd think you'd be ashamed to keep bothering me. I've played the starry-eyed romantic for nine long years . . . and what have I gotten out of it? Promises, that's what. A lot of phony promises to marry me . . ."

She ran out of breath for a moment. A voice drawled in her ear. "You've sure got your dander up about something, honey."

Carol froze. It wasn't Jerry. She had just bared her soul to a stranger.

"Who is this please?" she asked stiffly.

"Paul Gordon. I believe you're supposed to show me a house . . . ?"

PUT PLEASURE IN YOUR READING Larger type makes the difference This EASY EYE Edition is set in large, clear type—at least 30 percent larger than usual. It is printed on scientifically tinted non-glare paper for better contrast and less eyestrain.

Honeymoon House
Florence Stuart

VALENTINE BOOKS
NEW YORK

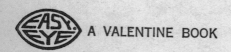 A VALENTINE BOOK

HONEYMOON HOUSE

Copyright © 1962 by Arcadia House
All rights reserved
Printed in the U.S.A.

Valentine Books are published by
PRESTIGE BOOKS, INC., 18 EAST 41ST STREET
NEW YORK, N.Y. 10017

Chapter One

Carol Kane couldn't believe her own ears as she heard Jerry's voice over the phone. "Please don't be angry at me, honey, but I'm afraid we'll have to postpone our plans again. Something pretty terrific has come up and—"

She sat up, swung her legs over the bed and started to boil. On the chair beside the bed was a white cashmere dress with a fur jacket that was to have been her wedding outfit. She glared at it. She thought of her bridal corsage, tucked away on ice in the refrigerator. She took note of the bright golden October California sun streaming through the window by her bed.

Such a lovely day to be married.

Also such a lovely day *not* to be married, she thought, recalling the last time Jerry had let her down at the last minute. That day the fog had been rolling in, and the time before that—

"Are you still there, dear?" Jerry sounded as casual as if he'd just phoned to break a movie date for that night.

"No!" Carol snapped. "I've gone into orbit. Maybe in outer space I can find a man whose promises mean something."

"Don't be like that, honey. Give me a chance to explain this deal that's come up. Have you read about a guy named Paul Gordon who just inherited part of the John Gordon hotel fortune?"

Well, why am I so surprised? Carol asked herself as she drew a blue robe over her shoulders. How often do I have to find out, the hard way, that Jerry doesn't want to marry me? What he really wants is to keep me as his little office slavey. I'm a convenience for him, that's all.

I'd be a nice convenience for any ambitious young Hollywood architect. Private secretary, office girl, interior decorator, file clerk, cleaning woman in a pinch—and I'll turn my hand to any other odd jobs that need doing.

Why shouldn't he promise to marry me every so often, just to make sure my ever loving heart doesn't run out on him? Because if it ever did,

6

he'd have a hard time finding another Jackie of half a dozen trades to work for the salary of one.

"I've never heard of Paul Gordon," she said, and stood up, slipping one foot into a satin mule, then the other. "I'm not interested in Paul Gordon or in the fortune he's inherited. Lots of people inherit fortunes, and I couldn't care less. All that interests me at the moment is that you've let me down again. The last time it happened, Jerry, I warned you. I told you if you ever do this to me again—"

"You're being very unreasonable, Carol."

"You gave me your solemn promise that today —this particular Saturday—we'd drive to Arizona, get married and take a week off for a honeymoon in Palm Springs. You promised me, Jerry. What's unreasonable about expecting you to keep your promise?"

"You're twisting things around, as usual," Jerry said, "to put me in the wrong." And he made it sound as if he really were the one who was being imposed upon. "You know perfectly well that we can get married some other time. There are other weekends."

"Oh, sure." She was wild with anger, with hurt pride, with the hurt in her heart. Only this time her heart seemed to be taking the blow better than the rest of her. Maybe hearts got used to being walked over every so often. But her hurt pride wasn't going to get used to it, wasn't taking any more.

"Sure, Jerry. There'll still be plenty of weekends coming up, even when I'm ready to totter into a Home for the Aged." And before that, of course, long before that, she'd start growing older and older, slowly turning into one of those dreary, pathetic, bedraggled old creatures who had spent the best years of her life being hopelessly in love with the boss, who never got around to marrying her.

"As I was saying," Jerry repeated himself, "there'll be other chances to marry, but this Paul Gordon thing may mean the kind of opportunity which comes but once. He's looking for a house for himself and his bride. I figure I may get him interested in our Honeymoon House. If I can do that, something else may follow; something *big*."

"So now Paul Gordon has a bride." Carol gave an elaborate sigh. "Well, good for her. I'm so glad for her. A man promised to marry her and actually went through with it."

"They aren't married yet," Jerry said. "It's just in the works. First they've got to buy a house."

"Oh. Well, I hope the girl never finds herself where I am: wondering whether to pitch her bridal corsage in the garbage can or to toss it to the birds."

8

"Carol, you've got to listen to me. You've got to be reasonable about this thing."

"You said that before, Jerry. There's something I've said before, too. I said if you ever did this to me again, I was through. I meant it. I am."

She was still seething as she hung up.

For a minute or two she just stood there, staring at the floor. It was like finishing a book, she thought; a book with a disappointing ending about a heroine who had wasted nearly ten years of her life mooning and dreaming romantic dreams about a man who had simply used her for a convenience.

Yet that wasn't altogether true about Jerry. In the beginning he hadn't been like that. Not in the days when he used to come to her dad's house, along with a swarm of other UCLA students who regarded her father more as a friend than as a professor. Of course, if they wanted or needed advice, he had been a wise, understanding man with good advice to give.

But if they were simply lonely boys who wanted friendship from this older, gentle man, Professor Kane gave them that, along with an easy chair by the open fire, good strong coffee, and all the cookies they could eat. Carol, sixteen at the time, passed around the coffee and cookies.

And when Jerry came, a tall, dark, handsome, gifted boy of twenty, she passed him her heart as well. That was when it all started; when she was sixteen. She was now twenty-five, would be twenty-six in another two months. And in all the years since she had never given a serious thought to any other man, never known a heartache over any man but Jerry. She had been so sure, right at the start, that he was the right one for her. She could still remember how she had absolutely ached with love for him, back in those long ago days. And maybe he had been worth it—then.

Maybe he had loved her, too—at the time.

For when he was twenty, Jerry had been a very different kind of person from the egotistical, money-greedy, high-pressure salesman he was today.

When he was twenty, all that he had wanted was to be an outstanding architect. That had been an end in itself. But somehow, during the years, he had changed. His love affair with money had begun, and the blueprints which cluttered the desk in his Wilshire Boulevard office were simply designs to make him a millionaire by the time he was thirty-five.

I'm not in love with him any more, Carol thought. It was a strange truth that came over her very suddenly, as she stood there gazing at the floor, trying to fight the anger over this latest blow to her pride. Perhaps she never had been in love with this thirty-year old man with his obsession for big business deals and making a lot of money. Her heart had simply once been caught and trapped by a shy, endearing boy who hadn't existed for a long, long time.

"Well, it's all over now. I'm free of it at last." Hearing herself say the words aloud gave her a happy, lighthearted feeling, and she was actually laughing as she headed for the bathroom.

While she was standing under the cold shower spray, the phone rang again. She ignored it.

It would be Jerry calling her back. She didn't want to talk to him, was in no mood to listen to any more of his raving about the big deal he was cooking up in his mind. He'd ruined her day, not to mention what he'd done to several years of her life. Was it too much to ask that he let her alone— for a few hours, anyway?

Three more times the phone rang: once while she was waiting for the coffee to perk, again while she was drinking her first cup. The third time she gave in.

"All right," she said into the receiver. "What is it now, Jerry? If you think you can talk me into driving to the office today, you might as well save your breath."

"Listen, honey."

And for a solid five minutes Jerry talked. He seemed to imagine she was a promising prospect

11

to whom he was giving the high-pressure treatment.

She knew how badly he wanted to get rid of the Honeymoon House, which had been one of his few bad mistakes. "You know how much it means to me, honey. If I can just sell that little—"

"Horror," Carol interrupted. "That's the word for it, Jerry. I told you so before you ever built it. Didn't I tell you it would never sell?" To be honest, horror wasn't quite the word for the little hilltop house, which really did have a magnificent view, and enough glass to wall in all the fish in the Pacific. The main trouble was that it belonged in the twenty-first century, not the twentieth. People still wanted *homes* to live in, not electronically controlled fish bowls.

Yes, she'd told him. Jerry conceded that much. Hindsight was better than foresight, and so on. But the house was built, he had it on his hands, so the thing to do was to find a sucker who would buy it. Maybe this Paul Gordon was the sucker he was hoping for. That would take care of the house itself, but there was more to it that that. There were those thirty acres of land surrounding Honeymoon House.

"I've taken an option on that land," Jerry said, and Carol wouldn't have been more surprised if he'd told her he'd made a reservation for the first flight to the moon.

"You've *what?*" That land, on the outskirts of Hollywood, would cost a small fortune. Jerry didn't have that kind of money, and she couldn't think of anyone who would advance it.

Last night, Jerry explained, right after he had the phone call from Paul Gordon, he had gotten in touch with the real estate firm that had the thirty acres for sale. He had taken a thirty-day option on it. The way he figured it, if Paul Gordon could be talked into buying the house, he could be talked into putting up the money for the land around it.

"And use it for what?" Carol asked pleasantly. "Cattle grazing?"

Jerry missed the humor of that remark. "We could build about fifty of these houses and sell them to newlyweds. We'd call it Honeymoon Villa. You know, they have villas for Senior Citizens. *That* idea has swept the country like wildfire. Some guy has made three or four fortunes from it. So why not sell the same idea to the kids who are just starting out in life?"

"Sure. Why not? Why not call it Love Birds' Villa?" Carol suggested sweetly, and was astonished when she heard Jerry saying in all seriousness: "Now there's an idea."

What had happened to the man's sense of humor?

"Look, Jerry," she said. "This was to have been my wedding day: the day I've dreamed about,

13

planned for, lived for. Thanks to you, the bottom has dropped out of every dream and plan I ever had. Well, I'm not going to blow my brains out because you don't really want to marry me, and probably never did. But I do have a little readjusting to do. I have my own life to think about. I simply haven't the time to bother any more about you or one of your big deals."

"But you're in on this, Carol. I need your help."

"That's too bad, Jerry, because my help you're not getting. Go find yourself another slavey." And for the second time that morning she hung up on him.

She spent the next hour straightening up the cottage. It was a sweet little place. White-shingled and green-shuttered, it looked as if it might have been flown straight from New England and set down there in the shadows of the Sierra Madre foothills. Inside, it was all hooked rugs and maple pieces. A few of the pieces, including the cobbler's bench in front of her stone fireplace, were genuine antiques. It had an old-fashioned look, and Carol loved it for that very reason. She had planned to put it up for sale as soon as she returned from the honeymoon.

It was a lucky thing she had waited.

Now she would keep the cottage and go right on living here until her life took some turn that she couldn't at the moment foresee.

14

What, for instance? she wondered, standing before her mirror. The mirror couldn't have been kinder. It showed her a tall, slender girl with a mass of blue-black hair that had a lovely natural wave. Her eyes were such a deep blue they looked almost black, and they were set in a high-boned face that was altogether lovely.

She stood there for a minute or two studying herself. It had never occurred to her to wonder if she might fall in love with some other man, or some other man with her. She had been too busy being in love with Jerry. But a girl couldn't help wondering when she suddenly found herself at loose ends. Maybe there was somebody else somewhere, she thought now. Somebody she could laugh with, talk with, learn to love in a quiet, tender sort of way. Somebody who would feel the same way about her and want to live with her, to grow old with her. It gave her a dull ache, a feeling of sadness to think she might never find *anyone*. She didn't want to live alone and unloved, not needed by anybody, for the rest of her life.

The phone rang once more.

She hadn't the slightest doubt that it was Jerry again, and all the sadness and loneliness she had been feeling mingled with the biting anger that was still eating at her. The net result was a wild, bitter, consuming rage. She felt bursting with it as she grabbed up the receiver. Without giving him

15

time to say a word, all her pent-up feelings were loosed in a storm of words that came as fast and furious as angry water rushing through a broken dam.

"After what you've done, Jerry Powers, I'd think you'd be ashamed to keep bothering me. When I told you I was through, I meant every word of it. For ten long years I've played the starry-eyed little romantic who couldn't see I was being used for a good thing. I helped you through college. I talked dad into giving you special coaching to help you finish four years work in three. And after he died I loaned you money from his estate to open your office. Then I went to work for you, and if I do say it myself, I've helped you put over quite a few deals that would have gone down the drain without me. And what have I gotten out of it? Promises, that's what. A lot of phony promises to marry me; some more promises to love me forever when the fact is you've never loved me at all."

She ran out of breath for a moment. There was not a word from Jerry during her brief silent pause, so she took up where she had left off. Only now her voice was calmer, edged with sadness.

"Oh, I'm not blaming you for not loving me, Jerry. Why should I? The reason is terribly simple. We just aren't the same kind of people. Once we were, or at least I think we were. But not any more. We don't want the same things from life. All you really care about is making a lot of money. All I really want is a home, a nice little family, and a man who thinks I'm the most important thing in the world to come home to." Her voice suddenly broke on a sob. "Well, I guess that covers it, Jerry. Can't you see there's no use to keep phoning me? I'm through, Jerry, honestly."

"You've just got your dander up about something or other, honey," the voice said. "This character can't be as big a heel as you're making him sound. It stands to reason, if you've loved him like crazy all this time, that there must be *some* good in him. Wait until you simmer down; then think things over. That's my advice, honey. By the way, are you Miss Carol Kane?"

Carol's eyes took on a glazed look. Obviously, the receiver in her hand wasn't a snake, but she looked at it as if it were. This was horrible. She had bared the secrets of her very soul to somebody who wasn't Jerry!

She shuddered. "Who is this, please?" She managed the words with perfect calm, with as much cool poise as if she hadn't just finished making a perfect idiot of herself.

"The name is Paul Gordon. I'm calling from a public phone right here in Sierra Madre. I was wondering—would it be okay if I drop around to see you for a few minutes?"

17

"I'd be ashamed to face you, Mr. Gordon," Carol said. "I don't often lose my temper, but when I do—"

"When you do, you really tell a guy off, don't you?" He had a nice warm, friendly laugh. "I'm the same way myself. I keep it all bottled up until suddenly the cork pops out, and then, *wham*. You wouldn't recognize me as my usual calm, easygoing self. Well, how about twenty minutes from now?"

"I'm afraid not, Mr. Gordon." But little good it did to say it, because she was talking to a dead line.

Chapter Two

I simply cannot face the man, she thought, as she stripped off her housecoat.

She wouldn't let him inside the house, she decided.

She would make him stand outside while she gave him her unabridged opinion of a man who listened to extremely private words that were not intended for his ears. She would make him feel so thoroughly ashamed of himself that he would turn around and leave at once.

But while she was telling him off, she might just as well look her best. She'd let the man see she wasn't the pitiful, broken-hearted creature she must have sounded over the phone.

So she decided on the most becoming dress she

owned. It was of coral-pink angora wool, and it was stunning with her black hair and her deep blue eyes. She put on earrings that went with the dress, lipstick the exact shade of the earrings. It was a little like dressing up to act out a scene in a play. It hadn't occurred to her as yet to wonder what he wanted to see her about, or how he had gotten her phone number, or knew where she lived, or had learned her name, or even that she existed.

The knocker sounded. She went to the door. Her head was high, her voice icy. "It isn't convenient for me to invite you in, Mr. Gordon. But now that you're here, there's one thing I'd like to say. I am very sorry if I gave you a wrong impression about myself. As a rule, I keep my emotions under control. I do not fly off the handle like a screaming banshee every time something happens to irritate me. I mean, Mr. Gordon, ordinarily I act and sound like a girl with good sense. Of course I didn't realize that my words were being broadcast to a stranger with extremely bad manners. Didn't your mother ever teach you, Mr. Gordon, not to listen in on the private affairs of other people?"

There, she thought. That was telling him, in a nice, dignified way, exactly what she thought of him. "You don't *look* like a snooping eavesdropper," she said, after the moment of silence became a little embarrassing.

Why didn't the man say something? Did he think all he had to do was stand there, giving her that slow, friendly smile, and she'd weaken and let him come in?

He was tall and rangy, with a lot of reddish brown hair and bright blue eyes with quiet laughter in them. *Was he laughing at her?* The thought made her furious, and she burst out: "Why don't you say something, Mr. Gordon?"

"What do you want me to say, honey?" His slow, Texas drawl probably explained the "honey," Texans called everybody honey, even doddering old ladies, she'd heard.

"Well, you might apologize. Don't you think you owe me an apology, Mr. Gordon?" She grabbed a quick breath. "After all, you could have hung up the phone, couldn't you, when you realized I thought I was talking to some other man?"

"Maybe so." He was still grinning. "But I'm a guy with a curious mind, so I was real curious to hear what you were going to say next. And I certainly was thankful I wasn't the other man. I'd sure hate to have a beautiful girl go at me, hammer and tongs, the way you were going at him."

"You owe me an apology."

"Okay, honey. If you say so. I apologize most humbly."

21

"You ought to be ashamed of yourself."

"I am. My head is bowed in shame. I'm a heel. My dad should have taken me on more trips to the woodshed when I was a kid. I don't see how I'm to live with myself from now on. Every time I take a look in the mirror, I'll say, 'you cad.' That's what I think of myself. Now may I come in, Miss Kane? Please?"

"No!"

So a few minutes later he was seated on the lounge in her living room. She asked him if he'd like a cup of coffee. He sure would, Paul said. And while she was fixing the coffee, would it be okay if he used her phone?

Carol showed him where it was in the bedroom, dashed back to the kitchen, and while she waited for the water to boil decided she saw no reason she shouldn't do a bit of prying into his love life. Turn about was fair play, wasn't it?

So she tiptoed into the hall and listened to him saying about a thousand times: "Well, I'm sure sorry to hear you're still feeling poorly, Susan, honey. . . . Have you taken a lot of aspirin, honey? . . . I understand, honey; I know all this house hunting has worn you out, and I'm to blame. I'll tell you what I'm going to do, Baby Doll. This time I'm going to get another girl to act as a kind of stand-in for you. I guess all you gals are a lot alike when it comes to choosing houses. So I'm

22

going to try it out on this other girl, get *her* viewpoint. That way you won't have to wear out your poor little feet trudging from one place to another. Now you just take it easy, Susan honey. Give my love to your mother, and—"

Well! Carol thought.

So he was going to use her as a stand-in, was he?

Another man figuring he could use her for a convenience.

She tiptoed back to the kitchen, poured the coffee and went back to the living room with fire in her eye.

"Wonderful coffee," he said.

"Thank you," Carol said.

Now would he mind answering a few questions?

It was all very simple, Paul explained. He had been on the phone half a dozen times, talking to Jerry Powers, who claimed that he had a perfect little gem of a house that would give a big thrill to any bride-to-be. Jerry had wanted to show them the house that afternoon. But the trouble was, Paul said, his little Miss Apple Blossoms had already looked at about two hundred houses in and around Hollywood, and her feet had given out on her. What was more, she had caught some kind of a virus. And in addition to all that, she had a bad headache.

"The poor thing seems to be in pretty bad shape," Carol said. "It's not surprising. How does she manage to live at all—with a name like Apple Blossoms?"

Paul grinned. "Oh, that isn't her real name. Susan—Susan Starr, that is—is a very pretty little gal who was crowned Miss Apple Blossoms a few months ago, back in Virginia. So that's one of my pet names for her."

"Oh, one of those things."

Paul stared at her for a minute; then he burst out laughing. "I know exactly what you're thinking, Carol, and I couldn't agree more. I've always figured beauty prize stunts were strictly for the birds. But in this case, Susan isn't really to blame. She's a nice, sweet kid with a mother who won't let her call her soul her own. Mama high-pressured her into entering this contest."

"I see." Immediately she saw an ambitious mother nosing out a newly made millionaire as a heaven-sent husband for pretty little Susan. Paul Gordon didn't look the slightest bit like a wealthy man. That, of course, was a silly thing to come into her mind. Why should a rich man look any different from a poor man? Well, there was the matter of clothes. Paul was wearing gray slacks and a leather jacket over a plaid sports shirt. There was nothing wrong with any of them. They just didn't look as if they'd been flown, air mail, from Brooks Bros. in New York. And his Chevy, outside by the curb, was definitely a five- or six-year-old model.

He hasn't blown his top, Carol thought, just because he's inherited a little money. And in contrast she thought of Jerry.

If Jerry Powers suddenly came into big money, he'd be racing around town in an imported car, wearing imported tweeds, handing out five-dollar tips for a dollar lunch.

"I only hope her mother isn't pressuring her into marrying me." It was the first time a gloomy note had come into his voice. "It sort of worries me." He looked up, meeting Carol's eyes across the room. "Susan is such a sweet little kid." He made it sound as if she were about eight, going on nine. "I'd hate her to be pushed into marrying me. How can a man tell about a thing like that?"

He looked worried.

"Does she say she loves you?"

"Well, yes and no."

"I see. Well, why not set a date for the wedding?" Carol suggested sweetly. "When the time comes, think up some flimsy excuse to back out at the last minute. Maybe you have to dash somewhere to a dying aunt's bedside. If she cries her eyes out, loses her appetite, goes for long solitary walks, and finally swallows fifty or so sleeping tablets, she loves you. If she just flies off the handle, tells you off, then orders you to go get lost forever-more, you'll know she's really thankful to be rid of you."

His eyes on her were thoughtful. "Is that the way it is with you, Carol?"

She froze. "It's *your* love life we were discussing, not mine. Now about the house problem: I take it that Jerry Powers gave you my name and phone number. Why? *He* designed and built the house. He can tell you everything there is to know about it. Why did he send you to me?"

"Because I told him I'd like a girl to look over the house with me when I went to see it." Susan had her tender, aching feet, as well as shot nerves. She didn't seem to be up to any more house hunting.

The poor girl had become practically hysterical after the last trip to see a house which didn't suit her at all. He had had a terrible time calming her down. All of a sudden she detested every house in Hollywood, she detested Hollywood itself, she wished she'd never left Virginia. "She even threatened to kill herself."

"She seems to be an excitable little thing."

"Yes. I guess maybe it was this virus in her system. Anyway, I decided the thing to do was to get some woman's viewpoint on this next house before I bother Susan about it. So your friend, Jerry, told me to get in touch with you right away. He

26

said you knew everything there was to know about this particular house: *Honeymoon House.* Is that what he called it?"

"He probably did," Carol said. "Jerry should be in the advertising business," she added dryly. "He believes a catchy tag name will sell anything, and he's very good at thinking up names. What else did he say about me? And oh, by the way, did he mention anything about the land adjoining the house?"

Yes, Paul said, he had mentioned something about quite a few acres of the best building land left in this part of the world.

"He said," Paul continued, "that you took the psychological approach toward selling houses, that you believed a house that was perfect for one person could be all wrong for another. Well, that's exactly what I want to know, Carol. Would this house we're talking about be the right one for Susan, or wouldn't it?"

Carol studied him for a moment. "Suppose you tell me a little more about Susan," she said carefully. "So far, all I know is that she won a beauty prize, she has a domineering mother, she gets crying spells when she's tired out. That's scarcely enough to help me decide what kind of a house she'd be happy in."

It had been her opinion for a long time that the average, otherwise reasonably intelligent man regressed into a backward state once he became infatuated with a beautiful face. Paul Gordon's raving during the next ten minutes or so did nothing to change her mind on that point.

He finally shook his head. "When that little gal looks at you out of those big, shining, dreamy eyes—" He implied that the whole question of Susan's loveliness was a subject to be approached with reverence.

"You never saw such a beautiful girl," he said. "I just can't begin to tell you."

As far as Carol was concerned, she had heard more than enough. It was downright sickening, to have to sit and listen to a bewitched man practically drool over the beauty of some teen-aged kid who was probably just another doll-faced girl with her eye on the main chance.

"Why bother about buying a house at all?" Carol inquired pleasantly. "Why not simply buy a gold frame and put her in it? Such a ravishing creature as you describe must have been designed for finer things than washing dishes or running a vacuum cleaner."

"Yeah," Paul said, looking worried. "You have a point there." Was Susan ready to be a wife?

It was a thing that had been bothering him considerably. He frowned morosely at the floor. He'd grown up on a Texas ranch. If he had his choice, he'd spend the rest of his days in the wide open spaces. Sometimes he wished he'd never inherited a lot of money from his rich uncle.

Paul lit a cigarette. He raised his eyes to stare hard at Carol, who was having a hard time making him out. One minute the man sounded as if he were blessed among men to have found his beauteous Susan. The next he sounded all mixed up and pretty doubtful about the whole thing.

A lot of unexpected money, he said, complicated a man's life no end. First, he had come to Los Angeles to straighten out some legal details in connection with his inheritance.

Then somebody had taken him to a Hollywood party.

At the party he had met Susan Starr, who was, without question the most beautiful girl he had ever seen.

"You said that before," Carol interrupted. "I think we can consider that point settled. Your Susan has the kind of face that launched a thousand ships."

"She isn't beautiful in the same way that you are beautiful," Paul said unexpectedly. He made it sound as if a very surprising thought had suddenly exploded in his brain. Carol reminded him coolly that *her* beauty was not under discussion. Furthermore, she was not beautiful, and she didn't care to be compared with a girl who was. This remark, innocent enough in itself, immediately led to a heated argument.

Paul insisted with passionate intensity that Carol, too, in her own particular way was one of the most beautiful girls he had ever seen. "I don't go for lying flattery," she told him back. When he swore that it was no lie, Carol laughed in disbelief. She told him that she'd been flattered by experts; it was what a man did when he wanted to get around her for one reason or another.

Finally she told him curtly: "You came here to talk business, Mr. Gordon. Let's confine our remarks to business. Let's keep the color of my eyes out of it, if you don't mind." She poured more coffee.

He was grinning at her again. "What are you getting so sore about, honey? All I started to say was, your eyes happen to be the deepest, darkest blue I've ever gazed at."

"Well, stop gazing at them!"

"It also just happens that I've always favored blue-eyed women. Now you take my mother. She had deep, velvety, tender blue eyes. A lot like yours, my mother's eyes were. Then there was this little gal I had a crush on when I was fifteen. *She* had blue eyes. Ella Mae was her name. I all but flunked out my second year in high, all because I was so upset about Ella Mae's beautiful blue eyes." He was still grinning. "Didn't know whether I was going or coming."

He sounded to her like a man who still didn't know whether he was going or coming. "We were talking about this house and whether it would be suitable for your Susan," she reminded him.

She had asked him to tell her something about the girl, and all he seemed able to tell was that she was a beautiful little redhead. Perhaps there was nothing more to tell, really. There were a lot of pretty girls like that; girls who had never had a real thought or experienced an honest emotion; girls whose entire lives revolved around their complexion and hair and slim little figures. Of course, they had to have the admiration of men to feed their vanity. And that was all there was to them, absolutely all. It seemed sad that this Paul Gordon might be going to settle for a girl like that.

Still he had his millions, and Susan had her beauty. Maybe it would make a good combination, and in any case, it was no concern of hers.

"Mr. Gordon," she said abruptly, "I don't think there's any use in you looking at Honeymoon House. It would simply be a waste of time and energy for both of us."

"What makes you say that, honey?"

"Because."

He grinned. "That makes everything perfectly clear."

All right, she snapped, if he insisted on details, the house in question was a novelty house. It was filled with all sorts of gadgets that would do practically everything except play a church organ and preach a sermon. To be honest, Jerry had taken the idea from a picture previewing what houses would be like in the next century. Jerry was an excellent architect, really brilliant. But sometimes he got so completely carried away with some novel idea that his enthusiasm blinded him to practical considerations. "I can't imagine a Texas rancher like yourself living in this house, Mr. Gordon," she said. "And frankly, from what you tell me about your Susan, I can't imagine her being bothered with *any* house. Why don't you settle for a hotel apartment, Mr. Gordon?"

"I wish you'd call me Paul," he said. And then: "She isn't *my* Susan—yet." He sounded sort of hopeful, but whether that meant he was hopeful she would be his or that she wouldn't be, Carol couldn't decide.

"I think I'd like to take a look at the house," he said after a moment.

She might have known. He was the stubborn type. Tell him a certain piece of property was all wrong, and right away he let you know that he, not you, was the one to decide that question.

It was a relief to hear the phone ringing.

She stood up.

32

She couldn't have been more blunt, more emphatic. "If you insist on seeing this house, Mr. Gordon, I suggest that you go back to Jerry Powers. He'll drive you out to it. I happen to have some personal problems on my mind right now. I have neither the time nor the inclination to bother showing you a property that I think would be a ridiculous buy for a man like yourself. I wouldn't even want to sell it to you. I don't believe in pushing sales that I consider all wrong. I don't think it's ethical."

"What you really mean is: you're sore at Jerry Powers who spoiled your wedding plans. Maybe you figure you can get even by spoiling a sale for him." And when Carol said: "How dare you drag my personal affairs into this?" he infuriated her by saying: "Because you're as transparent as glass."

The friendly smile was gone and his voice had lost its warmth. "If you want to be treated like an efficient business girl, you ought to act like one. But you're not. You're behaving like a spoiled brat who's been deprived of something she's set her heart on. If this fellow let you down, I don't blame you for being annoyed with him. But why take it out on me? And incidentally, why eat your heart out over a man who considers a business deal more important than marrying the girl he loves?

"What would you want with a man like that?"

It was the sheer impudence of it, the veiled contempt behind his words, that made Carol turn on him in a fury.

The phone was still ringing, but she disregarded that. "Just because you've inherited a lot of money, do you think that gives you the right to walk in here and speak your piece about my personal affairs? How would you like me to tell you what I think of a thirty-year-old man who goes overboard for a pretty teenaged girl who is probably after his money? I might ask you the same question you just asked me: what would you want with a girl like that? But it's no affair of mine and—"

"I'd want her," Paul interrupted coolly, "only if I believed she wanted me and truly loved me. That's still the best measuring stick I know for a happy marriage. But if I discovered she was out to use me for a convenience, I'd want no part of her. And I wouldn't go around taking my spite out on the first innocent bystander who happened along."

"I'm not taking my spite out on you!"

"Oh, yes, you are. In an indirect way, that's exactly what you're doing. Jerry Powers is desperately anxious to make this sale. I know that as well as you do. I know a high-pressure salesman when I see one, and that's one reason I didn't want him to show me the house. I wouldn't take his

34

word for anything. I would take your word. Honesty sticks out all over you, and that's why—"

"You haven't any right to say that about Jerry." Abruptly her sympathies swung into reverse. "You don't know the first thing about Jerry Powers. If I've given you a wrong impression—"

"I know that he puts up a big front in his Wilshire Boulevard office, which is supposed to make a big impression on fellows like me—from a Texas ranch. And I'm fairly sure he isn't the kind of man who would have postponed his wedding plans if he hadn't happened to know I'd just inherited a few million dollars."

"So what's wrong with that?" Carol interrupted angrily. "You inherited your money; Jerry has to work for his. And if he doesn't cater to clients who have money to spend, how do you expect him to make any?"

She was having a hard time keeping her temper from erupting completely. Just why she should be defending Jerry so staunchly she didn't try to understand. As things stood, she owed him nothing. Just the same, she wasn't going to have him berated, his honesty questioned, and not come to his defense. It was a question of loyalty.

"Frankly, Carol, it's of no concern to me how Jerry Powers makes his money. But since you brought up the subject, how do you expect him to make any sales if you go all out to drive a prospective buyer away?"

The phone was ringing again.

"Okay," she said, with a deep, long drawn sigh. It was simpler to give in than to go on arguing about it. "I'll show you the house. I'll meet you at Jerry's office at two o'clock."

"Carol?" It was Jerry on the phone. "Did Paul Gordon get in touch with you?"

"Yes. He just left."

"Then you've talked with him. That's good, wonderful. I hope you laid it on thick about the house."

"I told him he'd be a fool to bother looking at it." A statement which Jerry took for one of her little jokes. "But he insisted. So I'm to meet him this afternoon at the office."

"Fine." She was to get to the office as soon as possible, because Jerry wanted to have a talk with her. He had a plan of campaign all worked out. "If we pull this deal off, baby, we'll be in the big money. Then I'll be all set to marry you."

"Will you indeed!" Carol gritted her teeth, hung up and considered taking the first plane to Alaska. She felt headachy, depressed, completely out of sorts and angry at everybody, including Paul Gordon.

Chapter Three

Susan Starr lay on the bed with the blue satin cover and scowled at the absolutely nauseating wall paper, so gay and joyous with about a million bluebirds in a state of suspended animation all over it. "Oh," her mother had said, when they first saw the bedroom with its blue drapes and blue rug, "a symphony in blue! What a perfect background for you, honey lamb." It was the kind of remark she had learned to expect from her mother, who regarded her beauty-prize winning daughter as a kind of precious jewel.

All of her mother's important decisions were now made with an eye to setting off her jewel to the best advantage. And never mind if her little jewel was on the verge of going into a decline because of her lonely, aching heart. Her mother had no pity for an aching heart if the heart in question was Susan's heart, and the quite possible terminal condition of decline tied up with "that Connor Boy" back in Virginia whom Mrs. Starr invariably referred to as if he were an obnoxious form of microbe.

The fact of the matter was, Susan thought, as she felt under her pillow to make sure the letter was still there, her mother didn't really care whether her life was worth living or not.

The fact of the matter was, she decided as she reached for an apple on the bedside table and bit into it thoughtfully, her beauty was a curse. You didn't need to live in olden times to be a slave put up on the auction block. All you needed was to be born a little prettier than average, and have a mother who wouldn't let you call your soul your own, and win a silly beauty prize that got you a free ticket to Hollywood, and that was it!

After that, things happened fast—and all of them bad.

Off you flew to Hollywood, where you met all sorts of strangers who bored you to death.

Then somebody (not to mention any names because she hated even to *think* ill of her own mother) wrote her some lies about how the only man she could ever possibly love was mad about a silly little blonde named Mabel Grainger whom Susan had never been able to stand.

After that, why should she have cared whether she lived or died?

Obviously there was nothing to live for.

If Bob Connor was planning to marry that stupid little blonde, who had buck teeth, her faith in men and love and all that jazz was eternally blasted. About the only thing she could think of that could possibly give her any enjoyment was to show that faithless Bob how little she cared.

And that was the reason it had seemed an absolute godsend when she had met a tall, lanky Texan who was terribly rich and a sweet, dear man, even if he was almost old enough to be her father. What did his age matter?

Naturally, if you were marrying for love, you wouldn't want some old relic who had already lived his best years.

But she was done with love!

She had known it; she had known the suffering of love; she would never know deep, true love again. When she married, *if* she married, the best she could ask for was a man who would be kind, gentle, understanding; a man with enough money to give her the superficial pleasures of life.

When Paul Gordon came loping over the horizon of her life, complete with gentleness, an understanding nature and scads of money, he seemed made to order.

So when Paul said, "How would you like to marry me, honey?" Susan said with forced gaiety: "It's an idea." And the next thing she knew, she was wearing a four-carat diamond on her left hand, and her mother was on her way west to make sure that all went well.

Quite naturally, before she boarded the plane, Mrs. Starr made sure that everyone in town had heard the wonderful news that her beautiful Susan was engaged to a millionaire.

Susan disposed of the apple core in a plastic basket beside the bed. Then, once again, she felt under the pillow. As always, just touching the envelope which *he* had handled and addressed filled her with pain and sadness.

She should have trusted him. That was one of the things he had written in his beautiful, beautiful letter which she would treasure to the day she died. She should have known better than to believe he'd lose his head over that silly Mabel who, with all due respect to the gal, was a man-crazy little dope and always had been. "How stupid can you get, Hideous?" That had always been one of Bob's pet names for her, dating back to when she was around twelve and probably had been a hideous little monster. "If you can believe I'd go off

40

my rocker over that little creep, what you need is to consult a head shrinker."

Susan put her head back on the pillow, feeling much as Camille must have felt right before the end. *Now* he writes me this letter, she thought, when it is forever too late.

Her mother came marching into the room. Molly Starr was five feet of concentrated drive and energy attached to a pair of fiery blue eyes and a disarmingly soft southern voice.

"How're you feeling, honey lamb?"

"My head hurts, Mother."

"My poor, blessed little love. Do you feel up to coming to the phone, precious? It's some real estate man. He sounds very nice."

Susan groaned. If she never heard the words "real estate" again as long as she lived, she would be able to die happy. "I'd like to spit on every real estate man in Hollywood!"

Molly's blue eyes widened with something akin to horror. "Dearest, you shouldn't say such things." She'd tried so hard to teach her child to be refined under any and all circumstances. "Spit is such an uncouth word."

"Your dentist says it all the time," Susan defended herself. Anyway, she was not going to talk over the phone to any real estate man.

Scowling darkly, she pulled the blue satin up

41

around her throat and watched her mother dart out of the room.

Seconds later Molly was back with the information that Mr. Powers would call back a little later. "He just wants to get acquainted with you, dear. He knows about your winning the beauty prize and all, and I suppose dear Paul Gordon has told him how lovely you are. Anyway, he wants to see you, and say hello, and maybe take you for a little drive if you'd care to go. He even mentioned introducing you to some famous screen star. I must say, he couldn't have been nicer—so thoughtful, so friendly, so eager to put himself out to make you feel at home in California. What are you scowling about?"

Susan looked defiant. "I'm not interested in getting acquainted with Mr. Powers. I don't want to go driving with him. I don't want to meet any screen star. Screen stars are just people, like anybody else."

"That's a fine way to talk, I must say. How often must I remind you, Susan? When people try to be friendly, you should meet them halfway."

"'I don't want to meet Mr. Powers halfway. All I ask of this Mr. Powers is that he let me alone."

She held her eyes closed as her mother came close and patted her cheek. "You'll get over it, dear. You think now that you won't, but you will."

Susan opened her eyes. "Get over what, Mother?" Her tone was sweet, her eyes belligerent.

"Oh, you know: love. Your foolish crush on that common, ordinary Connor boy." She sighed. "I thought that was all over and forgotten. I can't think what he could have written in that letter that came a day or so ago. You haven't been like yourself since. I was tempted not to give it to you, and maybe I shouldn't have.

"Really, Mother, is it necessary for you to use those two words when you refer to Bob Connor? There's nothing common or ordinary about him."

"That family is as common as dirt, Susan." Molly Starr's voice rose a full octave, and it had a decided rasp. "The mother has a little chicken farm, and the father runs a shoe repair shop. They're people with no ambition to better themselves! Do you think I'd want you to marry into a family like that?"

Susan sat up.

Her eyes were blazing. "Bob's people are just as good as you or me or anybody else. His father runs that shop because he has a heart condition and has to take things easy. What's more to the point, Bob is a smart boy. He has plenty of ambition. And we were in love with each other. Doesn't that mean anything at all to you, Mother, I loved him."

"Puppy love." She sneered. "A boy you became

43

infatuated with when you were a child. That's when I should have taken a hand. I should never have let that boy inside our house."

"Why did you lie to me, Mother? After I came out here to California, why did you write me that Bob was engaged to another girl? How could you do a thing like that to me? You knew it wasn't true."

"I knew nothing of the sort. It was common talk around town that Bob and Mabel Grainger were engaged. Mabel said it herself, not three weeks after Bob came home from college for his summer vacation. Anyway, what does it matter now? You're engaged to a perfectly wonderful man. You have a perfectly wonderful life ahead, You're one of the luckiest girls I ever heard of, Susan. I only hope you have sense enough to appreciate your good fortune in getting a man like Paul Gordon!"

"I just don't happen to love Paul, that's all."

Susan should have known better than to say that right out!

The torrent of words that issued from her mother's lips were the same words Susan had listened to a million or so times before. What did she want? To throw herself away on a common, ordinary boy who just possibly might get to be a small town lawyer one of these days?

"He'll never make anything to speak of. People

like the Connors never accumulate any money. They're satisfied to live from hand to mouth. Bob will be like all the rest of the Connors, and what kind of a life will his wife have?"

A life that would suit me just fine, Susan thought bleakly. Her hand crept under the pillow again, and her fingers touched the envelope with love, with longing.

"She'll be washing, cooking, cleaning, raising half a dozen or more redheaded children. The Connors *all* have redheaded children," proclaimed Molly, as if it were another point to prove the folly of the whole thing. "Six months of it, and you'd be wondering whatever happened to all the beautiful love you're bleating about."

Susan stared at her mother wonderingly. How was it possible, she wondered, for anybody to grow so old that she forgot how important love was? Her mother wasn't so terribly old. She was forty. That was pretty ancient, of course. Still, at forty surely there should still be some dim memory of how it had been when you were young and love was the most important thing in the world.

"And here you are," Molly continued, "practically a famous beauty, with a man like Paul Gordon at your feet! He's only too eager to shower you with gifts, to give you a life of ease. Married to Paul, you'll never know what it means to want for a single thing your heart desires. You will live in luxury, wear beautiful clothes, meet all sorts of interesting people. You can travel and see the world. You'll have all the things that I've wanted my life long and never had. And you lie there on that bed mooning over that Connor boy.

"Frankly, Susan, I'm completely out of patience with you."

"I'm sorry, Mother. But I can't help the way I feel, can I?"

"Of course you can help it! What you need to do is take hold of yourself. Get that Connor boy out of your head once and for all. Is Paul taking you to dinner this evening?"

"No, Mother."

"Why not?"

"I told him I wasn't feeling well. I have a headache, and I feel sort of dizzy when I stand up. I think I'm running a fever."

Her mother clamped a cool hand to Susan's forehead. "Nonsense. You haven't any more of a fever than I have. Now you mind what I say, Susan. You can't play fast and loose with a man like Paul. This may be your first, last and only chance to marry a rich man. Do you want him to slip through your fingers?"

Susan's only reply was a weary shrug. She stared some more at the bluebirds on the wall, while her mother stared at her. Apparently Molly Starr decided she'd had about all she could take of a daughter who didn't know which side her bread was buttered on. "I should never have let you have that letter," she said, and left the room.

Chapter Four

Susan listened carefully. The swinging door to the kitchen had a squeak. As soon as she heard it, she knew that her mother would be preparing a "dainty luncheon salad." Susan detested salads, dainty or otherwise. She had no plans to eat any lunch whatever. Her appetite was a thing of the past. But anything that would keep her mother busy in the kitchen for five or ten minutes was something to be thankful for.

She needed to be alone. She needed to think.

Even if everything did look absolutely hopeless, it never did any harm to think and brood. There was always the chance a ray of sunshine might show up when you least expected it, that you might have a clever idea that would offer a way out.

She was out of luck, because in less than two minutes by her watch—the fabulous diamond-studded watch which Paul had given her the week before, on her eighteenth birthday—she heard the click of her mother's heels headed back in her direction.

At a very early age, when she was no more than eight or nine, Susan had discovered that there was only one place in the world where her privacy was inviolate. That was in the bathroom, with the door locked, bolted if possible, and the water running full blast.

There, there alone, her mother couldn't intrude to aggravate her in one way or another. The sound of running, gurgling water was designed to drown out any revealing noises, such as the crackling pages of a secret letter which was for her eyes only. And there had always been such letters. Even when she was quite young, Susan had been the kind of girl who inspired weird poems and ardent notes.

By the time Molly Starr reached the bedroom, Susan had made her escape. The letter from under the pillow clutched in her hand, she flew to the adjoining bathroom, locked the door and turned on the tub spigot full blast.

"Are you ill, dear?"

"I'm all right, Mother," Susan shrieked back. "I just thought I'd take a bath."

"I'm not sure a warm tub bath is advisable, precious. It opens the pores. You don't want to get another cold on top of the one you have. Why don't you take a shower?"

"Because I prefer to take a tub bath, Mother."

"I see. Well, I wonder if it's wise, dear. You don't want to get the sniffles and a runny nose."

Susan was breathing hard. Something knotted inside her. Why couldn't her mother realize that she was grown up, that she was perfectly competent to decide simple matters for herself? She turned off the hot spigot.

"Mother," she said tightly, "if I'm old enough to get married, I'm old enough to take a bath without holding a family conference about it."

"That's a fine way to talk to your own mother who has only your best interests at heart." Molly was jiggling the doorknob. "Why do you have to lock this door, Susan?"

Susan sat on the edge of the tub, glaring at the door.

"If you'll unlock the door, I'll come in and scrub your back for you, dear, and give you a good, brisk toweling to make sure you're dry. Then you can jump back in bed and I'll give you an alcohol rub."

Susan didn't often lose her temper with her

mother, but she did now. Her words came out a scream. "I don't want my back scrubbed. I'm not a cripple, Mother. I can dry myself. Will you please go away and let me alone? That's all I want. Is that too much to ask? Just let me alone."

"Well, that's a fine way to talk," Mrs. Starr told her. "Frankly, Susan, I don't know what to make of you. You act so strange."

"Please let me alone!"

Silence descended.

Susan swallowed hard. She gritted her teeth and worked at a nail cuticle. She considered the tragedy of her life.

"Susan dear?" It was her mother's voice again. "Are you sure you're all right?"

"I'm perfectly all right, Mother."

"Well, if you're sure, I think I'll go out for half an hour or so. I have to go to the supermarket. And I want to get some of that nut bread you like at the bakery. I won't be gone long."

Susan drew a sigh of relief. Now she could skip back to bed, snuggle up against the pillows, and read her letter in peace.

Bob started out: "My dearest darling: Because you are my dearest, you always will be, even if you have decided to marry this rich old guy who will probably buy you ninety pairs of shoes and a sea-going yacht. Well, who am I to compete with that kind of green stuff? But I'd certainly like to know how you dreamed up this nightmare about me marrying Mabel Grainger."

This, of course, was in reply to the note Susan had written Bob, in which she had said sweetly: "Let me be the first to congratulate you, friend. Not that I can think of any reason to congratulate a man who desires to be stuck for life with that revolting Mabel. I'd have a hard time dreaming up a more horrible fate. Of course it's quite possible that Mabel has some terrific fascination which I've never happened to notice. Anyway, I hope you absolutely die of joy and happiness in Mabel's loving arms, and you might wish me the same. I'm going to marry the most fabulous man. He has more millions than he can count, and he's going to buy me a mansion with I don't know how many bathrooms and swimming pools and so on. However, despite the fact that I shall spend my future life wallowing in luxury, I shall never forget our adolescent romance. And I do hope you aren't too miserable with that buck-toothed blonde. I truly do. I remain your friend, and if you ever get out to California, do look me up. But don't bring Mabel along. Susan."

Bob dealt at some length with the matter of Mabel, whom he was *not* going to marry and had never considered marrying. Why did people go about spreading such a mean, malicious, ridiculous story?

For that matter, what had happened to Susan's head that she could bring herself to believe such a lie?

She *knew* she was the only girl he had ever loved, or would ever love.

Because he did love her, he'd never lift a finger to stop her from marrying a rich man who could give her the kind of life a sweet, beautiful, wonderful girl like herself rated.

"But I would like to see you once more, honey. I want to have that much to remember for the rest of my life. I want to memorize your sweet face. I want to make you understand that there'll never be anyone else for me. I want to say to you, while we're standing close: 'I love you, I always will.' Is that too much for a guy to ask? If I thought I could find a job out there, I'd be on the next plane. I wouldn't try to cut in on your romance with Old Moneybags or anything like that. I wouldn't make any trouble for you or embarrass you. But you're my girl and I want to see you again. If I thought I could find a job, I'd figure on staying out there and finishing up law at night school. Even if I never saw you after you were married, it would be a little something just to know we were living in the same town. It would be rough in a way; sure it would. But it would be sort of comforting, too. I guess you don't know anybody out there who would give me a job, do you? Any kind of an old job would suit me fine. Oh, honey, I want to see you so awfully bad. This thing has hit me worse than you'll ever know. I love you, love you, love you. Bob."

Having finished reading the letter, which she already knew by heart, Susan folded it back into the envelope.

She meditated.

How about telling Paul she had a cousin who was a very deserving young man and very anxious to find a job in California, because his health wasn't too good and his doctor had recommended the mild southern California climate?

Paul knew all sorts of people. He could find somebody a job easily. At first that struck her as a wonderful idea. Then she decided against it. She couldn't help it if she wasn't madly in love with Paul. But that wasn't any excuse for not playing fair, for lying to him.

You could like and admire and respect a man without loving him. She did like Paul Gordon, very much. And she wasn't going to try putting over on him. She wouldn't stoop that low.

She thought some more, becoming more and more depressed by the second. Everything seemed so hopeless.

She looked at her watch and decided to go out for a walk. While she was out, maybe she'd go to a fortune teller. There was one about five blocks

54

away on Hollywood Boulevard. She'd noticed the sign in the window: "Horoscope Readings. Your Future Foretold. Five Dollars."

She was slipping a sweater over her head when the phone rang.

She went to the living room, lifted the receiver, and a man's voice said: "Is this Miss Susan Starr?"

"Yes."

"Well, hello there, Susan. This is Jerry Powers speaking."

"I don't know any Jerry Powers," Susan said coldly.

"I know you don't know me, Beautiful. And that's what worries me. I want you to know me. What's more—"

"I'm an ill woman, Mr. Powers. I'm in no condition just now to look at any houses. So if that's what on your mind—"

"What's on my mind is that I want to get acquainted with a certain little beauty from Virginia. I've often heard it said that you've never seen how beautiful a woman can be until you've seen a Virginia beauty. I'd like to check up and see if it's true."

"You're quite a kidder, aren't you, Mr. Powers? Well, I don't happen to care to be kidded by somebody I've never laid eyes on. And as I just said, I'm not a well woman."

"I'm certainly sorry to hear that. What seems to be the matter, Beautiful?"

"I think it's an allergy, Mr. Powers. It's a thing that comes over me whenever some smart guy bothers me with a lot of silly remarks over the phone. I break out in red spots. Is there anything sensible you have to say? Because if there isn't—"

"How would you like to go for a drive, Miss Starr?"

"No, thank you."

"How about cocktails in one of the famous spots?"

"I never drink anything stronger than strawberry sodas." The remark brought a few tears to her eyes. Strawberry sodas! She must have had thousands of them, she and Bob, back at Morton's drug store at the corner of Church and Market Streets.

"Fine," Jerry said with hearty enthusiasm. "I used to be a strawberry soda man myself. Suppose I drive over and pick you up and we'll hunt up a soda. While we're gorging, maybe we can work out some little thing I can do to make you happy. Okay?"

"Thanks just the same," Susan said coldly, "but I don't happen to be in the mood for a soda at the moment."

Then a thought hit her!

With all the brilliance of a meteor flashing

across a darkened sky, an idea blazed in her troubled mind.

Feeding some glib fibs to Paul in order to use him for a secret purpose of her own would be dishonorable. But making use of this Jerry Powers character was something else again.

Why shouldn't she use this eager beaver to gain something she wanted?

"Mr. Powers?" That ought to get him, Susan thought, practically overcome with admiration of her sudden dulcet tone. "Perhaps I spoke too hastily." She laughed throatily. "I guess I've become too emotional about this house business. I've been shown so many houses I dislike, when a man tells me he's in real estate I immediately take a dislike to *him*. I shouldn't do that, should I?"

"I don't want you to take a dislike to me, Susie." He laughed heartily. "Why, I'm one of the best-hearted fellows you're ever likely to meet. The very last thing in my mind is to try to sell you a house. That isn't the idea. I'm just a normal, average guy who admires beautiful girls. I like to meet beautiful girls. Making a sale doesn't enter into it. You do believe that, don't you, Susie?"

If there was one thing she detested more than another it was a man who called her Susie.

And as for her believing he wasn't after a sale —how stupid did he imagine a girl from Virginia could be?

"Of course I believe you, Mr. Powers." Her voice practically throbbed with her trust in his every word. "And you did say you'd like to do me a little favor, didn't you?"

"You name it, Susie!" He was all enthusiasm. "What would you like me to do for you? Considering that you have a wonderful marriage coming up, I assume you aren't after a movie test. But if by any chance you are, I'll see what I can do."

"Oh, my, no, Mr. Powers. I don't know the first thing about acting. And even if I did, I wouldn't ask you to do anything *that* big. I wouldn't want to make a nuisance of myself." She laughed at the very thought of it. "But—well—" She hesitated, as if she were too shy to say what was on her mind.

Then: "Oh, I guess I'd better not say it, Mr. Powers. You'd think I had an awful nerve, trying to impose on your good nature and all."

"Aw, come on, Susie. Out with it." Again a hearty laugh. "I'm the kind of fellow who likes to do favors for other people. The way I look at it, the greatest pleasure a man can get out of this life is doing things to please another person, especially if the other person happens to be a stunning beauty who likes ice cream sodas."

Susan laughed gently. "My, you do sound like an awfully nice, kind man, Mr. Powers. You really do." And then she asked her favor.

58

There was a cousin back in Virginia who had been kind to her when she was a little girl. Cousin Bob wasn't a close cousin, she explained; just a sort of kissing cousin. But because he used to do so much for her, she wanted to do something nice for Cousin Bob. And Cousin Bob would give anything, absolutely anything, to come out to California if he was certain he could find a job when he got here. "So I was just wondering——"

Susan drew a quick breath, wondered if anybody would swallow that cousin stuff, and said: "Well, I happened to wonder if you'd know about any jobs lying around loose. Cousin Bob would take just about anything," she added quickly. "He's the kind who isn't afraid of work, and he can type, dig ditches, turn automobiles inside out, raise chickens. Oh, he can turn his hand to anything."

"So where's your problem, Susie?" asked Jerry Powers. "You just send that kissing cousin a wire to get himself out here, fast. There'll be a job waiting for him. Now tell me, do you have a dinner date? Because if you haven't, suppose we skip the soda. I'll buy you dinner instead. That will give us more time to discuss the line of work your cousin is best suited for. How does that sound to you?"

"I've no objections," Susan told him sweetly.

"Fine. I'll pick you up around seven o'clock."

They hung up.

59

At the end of the line, Jerry Powers rubbed his hands with an air of triumph. Now he was all set. Men paid for the houses he sold, but first the woman had to decide which house to buy. Since women were controlled by their emotions, the really perfect sales approach was an emotional approach. Now that he understood what made little Susie tick, how could he miss? All that malarkey about her dear, dear cousin—that was a laugh. Obviously the kid had a sweetie back home. She wanted a few more dates with this boy friend before she toddled to the altar with her millionaire. And more power to her. He was all for giving adolescent romance another hour or so to remember forever; especially when it would win him Susie's undying gratitude. For a grateful girl was a girl who would tell Paul Gordon to sign any contract Jerry wanted him to sign.

He laughed aloud. Oh, this was a ten strike.

Meanwhile, at her end of the dead line, Susan was laughing delightedly to herself. She hadn't felt so cheerful in weeks.

This was a miracle.

If anybody had asked her an hour before, she'd have said there wasn't a chance that she'd ever see Bob again. Now she was going to see him. It was simply a matter of going to the nearest telegraph office, wiring him to come, then figuring how she was to meet him without her mother knowing anything about it.

She felt very strongly now that a kindly fate was smiling upon her, and when fate took a notion to dole out a miracle or two, anything could happen.

Chapter Five

In gold lettering, in the center of the ceiling to floor glass window facing on Wilshire Boulevard, were the words: *Jerry Powers, Architect and Builder*. Originally, when he first opened the office, it had been simply, *Jerry Powers, Architect*. That was before Jerry began to see that he was missing out on the big money. Designing houses was all very well, but the fortunes in southern California real estate were being made by the men who built and sold.

So Jerry launched into the building business.

Then he discovered another interesting fact. Nine women out of ten, if they could afford it, liked to have an interior decorator "do" their pretty new houses for them. It was a mark of status, a nice thing to brag about at bridge parties. "My interior decorator," they liked to say.

Jerry thought it over. Obviously there was little or nothing to being a decorator. Any woman with a flair for colors and an eye for arranging furniture to the best advantage could bring it off. If she had dark coloring that gave her a faintly French look and a good figure that looked well in bright red slacks, so much the better.

So in due course, at the lower left hand corner of the window, there appeared the words: *Carol Kane, Interior Decorator*. When Carol objected that she didn't know the first thing about professional decorating, Jerry laughed her worries away. "Read some books," he told her. "If you haven't any ideas of your own, snitch some out of the magazines. Buy yourself some ropes of flashy beads, tie a bright scarf around your head, and a touch of a French accent wouldn't hurt."

"So you expect me to pretend I'm something I'm not. I don't believe in trying to fool people, Jerry."

"Why not? People like to be fooled. If they didn't like it, why would they swallow all the silly ads they see on TV? Oh, and another thing. When you send out bills, make them plenty big. If you don't charge a lot, people figure you can't be much good."

Carol had been so much in love in those days.

Her heart had belonged so completely to Jerry. Her entire life had revolved around his life, helping him get started in his profession, helping him get ahead, helping him make money. So she wouldn't let herself take too hard a look at his business ethics or question his basic integrity.

After all, she could study interior decorating, couldn't she? She could learn. And she had. As it turned out, she had a very definite artistic flair, and in the course of a few years she had built up a well deserved reputation. "Get Carol Kane to do your house. She's a wonder." Ever so many satisfied customers said exactly that.

But at the start, I was a phony, Carol thought, glancing at her name on the window as she parked her car and walked across the pavement toward the office door.

She went into the office. Jerry Powers sat at his desk. He was a handsome man with shiny dark hair and flashing eyes. He was wearing gray flannel slacks, a pale blue silk shirt. He had a deep tan and beautifully manicured nails.

"Hello, honey." He rose as Carol came in. Even though they worked together, Jerry never forgot that he was a man, she a woman, and that manners were manners. "You're looking absolutely marvelous," he said.

As a matter of fact, Carol did look very stunning. She wore a smart black dress with a wide

64

white bow at the throat, a small white feather hat, white gloves. "Thank you," she said coolly.

"I've never seen you look more beautiful, darling. Makes me half wish I'd taken you to Arizona today as we planned."

He made it sound like a cute little joke!

For a moment Carol stood there, staring at him, and for the first time she tried to picture Jerry as a husband and father; coming home to his family in the evening, whistling happily while he did all sorts of little chores and played with the kids. She couldn't picture it.

Jerry offered her a cigarette. He lit it with the gold lighter one of his infatuated women clients had given him for Christmas. Lots of his clients went overboard for Jerry's charm and good looks, especially the fiftyish ones who were bored with their husbands, bored with their lives. They wrote him silly letters, they sent him gifts . . . and Jerry added a few thousand dollars to the prices of the houses he was selling them.

Carol sat on the edge of his desk while she smoked the cigarette. She kept looking at him very thoughtfully, but she said little. Her silence made him uneasy.

"I know you're disappointed about today, honey." For the first time he spoke of their disrupted plans seriously, and in a tone of deep regret. "Well, I'm disappointed, too. But I'll make it up to you, sweetheart. You can depend on that."

"It's all over, Jerry." She couldn't have been more emphatic as she tapped off a cigarette ash in a little bronze tray. Her smile was cool, her tone casual. "The only reason I'm here right now is that Paul Gordon was so insistent. Nothing would do but that I must show him the house. He wouldn't take no for an answer and—well, he seems like a nice person. So I agreed to meet him here. But don't get any wrong ideas, Jerry. I'm only doing this to accommodate Mr. Gordon. It doesn't mean that I'm back working for you. I've had it, Jerry. I'm not having any more."

Jerry didn't believe a word of it. He smiled at her. He had gone back to his chair. Now he got up again and came over to her. He slipped his arms around her. "Don't be like that, honey," he said, and kissed her cheek.

"I really mean it, Jerry," she kept saying, and Jerry devoted a solid ten minutes to assuring her that she didn't mean a word she was saying. The office couldn't get along without her, and neither could he.

"We'll get married on Christmas day," he suggested, "and go to Hawaii for our honeymoon. How does that sound to you, darling?" He kissed her again.

"Just the way your promises always sound,"

66

Carol said: "very attractive. The only trouble is, I've listened to too many of them. You'll promise anything that suits your purposes at the moment. Keeping a promise is something else again."

She shook her head slowly.

"Do you want me to go on my knees and ask your forgiveness?" Jerry asked meekly.

"Heaven forbid," Carol said, and went back to her own office. This was simply a part of the main room, shut off by four Chinese screens. The wall behind her desk was covered with Chinese prints. On her desk was an antique Chinese mirror which wasn't really a mirror at all, although the smooth, gleaming brass on one side had once served as one. "How interesting," one client had said. "Did Chinese women use this for a mirror? Really?"

It made a good conversation piece.

Carol sat down at the desk. She wanted to run through her address book, in which she had the names of all the women on whose homes she had worked. A vague plan was forming in her mind. If she could get a loan from the bank, maybe she could open an interior decorating shop of her own. If she did, she would send out announcement cards to everyone on her list.

The trouble was, before attempting a venture of that sort, she should be filled with passionate enthusiasm. She should be practically on fire with energy, drive, impatience to get on with it. Unfortunately, at the moment, driving energy and enthusiasm seemed to be qualities she was lacking.

She rested her elbows on the desk and covered her face with her hands. She felt dead tired, like a person who had just come to the end of a long, hard race, only to find that the goal post wasn't there. She had been racing madly toward *nothing*. For ten long years she had been engaged in a race toward a life of eternal happiness with the man of her dreams, only to discover that Jerry was not the man of her dreams. He was, instead, a dream man she had made up out of her own needs and longings. There was all the difference in the world.

Now where was she to find the energy and the desire to start another race—toward something she didn't even imagine she wanted? I don't want to end up just a successful businesswoman, she thought gloomily.

She heard the phone on Jerry's desk ringing.

"Hello?" Jerry said. Then: "Oh, it's you, Susie! What's on your mind, honey? Don't tell me you're calling to break our dinner date. If you did, it would break my heart as well." Laughter in his voice. Then: "How's that again, honey?"

Carol raised her head. She listened. Her eyes were very, very thoughtful for a moment, then filled with puzzled amazement as she heard Jerry saying: "Don't give it another thought, Susie. Of course I understand. I know all about family

68

problems; cases where a mother takes a dislike to some relative and can't stand the sight of him. There's one in every family. Of course I'll arrange a place where you can have a nice private little visit with Cousin Bob when he gets here. Of course. . . . No, honey it won't be a bit of bother. It just so happens, the young lady who works in my office has a nice little house where you can take Cousin Bob. How's that again, honey? Oh, no. She won't mind a bit. I'll fix it right up. Nothing to it. See you later, Susie. We'll arrange all the details while we're eating dinner."

"What was that all about?" Carol asked.

Jerry stood by her desk, grinning at her. "That was Susan Starr. Her sweetie from the old home town is flying out here. I'm supposed to believe he's a cousin she wants to do a kind deed for. Naturally she wants a place where she can see him alone. She can't go to his hotel room, and her mama would let go with fireworks if she took him to their apartment. The way I figure it, she wants a place where they can kiss a fond farewell and shed a few farewell tears. You don't mind loaning your house for this sad parting, do you?"

Carol stared at him for quite a while before she said: "What are you up to now, Jerry?" There were times when Jerry's schemes were so devious and subtle that even she couldn't figure them out.

69

This was one of those times. "What are you trying to do? Break up Paul Gordon's marriage?"

Jerry stared at her in absolute horror.

"Good heavens, no. I want to hurry it up. What we want is for the fellow to make up his mind right away about buying this house. To do that, he has to put the pressure on little Susan to get married right away. But first we've got to put the pressure on him; make the man realize he may lose this lovely doll if he doesn't work fast. See what I'm getting at?"

"I haven't the faintest idea what you're getting at, Jerry. If I had to hazard a guess, I'd say you sound like a man who has been working too hard. Your mind seems to be going around in circles."

Jerry laughed good-naturedly. "Have another smoke, Carol." And he gave her one. "Now you just sit there and smoke and relax while I explain it to you."

Chapter Six

"What gives you the right to mix into the personal affairs of two strangers?" Carol demanded. Her eyes were blazing; her voice was tight.

Jerry had just finished giving her a detailed report of his phone conversation with Susan. As she listened to him, something seemed to explode in Carol's brain. Was there nothing he wouldn't resort to to put over a sale?

Laughing, he eased himself off her desk to push the screens back, giving himself more space to walk back and forth. He smoked. He gestured with his hands. All the time he was smiling or else laughing out loud. He seemed to find the whole situation terribly amusing.

"You take things too seriously," he informed

Carol. "Anyway, what's wrong with mixing into other people's affairs? When you're doing everyone concerned a good turn, that is. The way I look at it, this millionaire from Texas is the slow-moving kind. If somebody doesn't put a little pressure on him, he might lose his little Virginia beauty. The thing to do with a doll like that is grab her fast."

"It's still no business of yours, Jerry. And even if it were, will you kindly explain what you hope to accomplish by bringing this Virginia boy friend flying into the picture? Assuming Bob is an old boy friend," she added. "After all, the man might really be a cousin. People do have cousins," she said dryly. "The way I've heard it, Virginia people have thousands of relatives. They feed them and sleep them; sometimes they move in and stay for years! Just because *you* wouldn't lift a finger to do something nice for a relative unless you stood to make a nice, fat commission out of it doesn't prove that this Susan wouldn't, or that there isn't any Cousin Bob."

"Oh, nuts." Jerry grinned at her cheerfully. He worked at his plaid tie, the one flashy item in his otherwise quiet attire. "Don't play stupid, darling. And as f⸻ at I hope to accomplish—that's sim-
ple⸻ ing, I expect to earn Susan's undy-
⸻ 's fair to assume she's just a brain-
tty face."

"Why is it fair to assume that?" Carol interrupted. "Just because a girl is pretty enough to win a beauty prize, it doesn't necessarily follow that she has a retarded mentality. She had enough sense to land a rich man," she pointed out wryly. "And it only took her a month or two in Hollywood to do it."

"It didn't take a giant mentality to do that," Jerry retorted pleasantly. "That's her reward for being nice to look at. But I'll go this far with you: I haven't a doubt she was on the hunt for a rich husband. These prize-winning lovelies always are. Now that she's found him, I feel very sure she'll hang onto him."

"What makes you so sure about that, Jerry? Once she has a few dates with this cousin who isn't a cousin—" Carol interrupted herself to get up for a drink of water. She tossed the paper cup in a plastic basket.

"Frankly, Jerry, I think it's the silliest scheme I ever heard of. It's stupid. There's such a thing as romantic love. Had you forgotten? What makes you so sure Susan won't fly into this Bob's arms and decide she wants to stay there forever?"

She sat down at her desk again, clasped her hands tightly and found herself thinking: And suppose she did walk out on Paul Gordon? He wouldn't want her if she was only after his money. So then he'd be free. Her heart lurched strangely.

73

She looked up.

"Romantic love!" Jerry was leaning against her desk, a decided sneer in his voice. What did Carol think? That they were still living in the Civil War era, with a southern beauty, complete with hoop skirts, waiting coyly on the wide veranda for some dashing male to come riding up, swoop her up in his virile arms and carry her away on horseback?

"One trouble with you, Carol, you read too much romantic fiction." It was an amusing remark if ever she had heard one. She couldn't remember when she'd had time to read any fiction. She'd been too busy helping Jerry make his mark in the world. Dead tired when evening came, if she didn't have a dinner date with Jerry, she'd go home, fix a makeshift dinner out of odds and ends, take a hot bath and crawl wearily into bed.

On the rare occasions when she had a little surplus energy but no date, as often as not she'd spend the evening cleaning Jerry's bachelor apartment for him. She'd run the vacuum, change the sheets, put fresh towels in the bathroom, list his soiled things to be sent to the laundry, toss out wilted flowers and arrange fresh ones. On an average of once a week she did all this for him, in return for which Jerry would give her a warm kiss, assure her she was a girl in a million, and ask what he would ever do without her.

Jerry seemed to be giving her a little lecture on modern adolescents.

Girls these days, he assured her, took no serious stock in romantic love. The average girl learned, before she was out of rompers, that the thing to do was find a husband who could give her things: cars; a flashy home, complete with all the gadgets she saw in the ads; a mink stole. A man who couldn't do all this for her, and a lot more, wasn't worth considering seriously.

If her mother didn't teach her these things, her teachers did. Hadn't Carol heard about modern progressive education? "That's part of the idea, dear," he instructed her patiently. "Little girls are taught that romantic love belongs to the dark ages. If they want to become properly adjusted to modern living, they must have all the lovely, expensive things that modern life and scientific ingenuity can give them. That means buy, buy, buy everything in sight, with plenty more coming up. To do that, obviously they must go out loaded for bear: in this case, a man who can write nice fat checks and keep on writing them."

Carol smiled at him pityingly. "In other words, you think every young girl is out to catch a rich husband. If she doesn't, she's a failure in life."

"Exactly. Which gets us back to Susan."

"Sure. Let's get back to Susan. Shall I say it for you? You imagine this Susan Starr would rather

75

shoot herself than let Paul Gordon get away from her. You think she wants to see her home town boy friend once or twice, maybe go dancing with him, and that will be that. Since the boy friend is poor, with his way to make—and Paul Gordon is loaded with his uncle's money—there's no question in your mind which one our Susan will settle on. Right?"

"Absolutely right," said Jerry, with the satisfied smile of a man who approached all such questions from a practical viewpoint. So how could he be wrong?

"I don't happen to agree with you," Carol said. "I think it's perfectly possible that Susan Starr might give you an extremely unpleasant surprise. But say you're one hundred percent right, just for the sake of argument. Let's say all she wants from Cousin Bob is a thrill, for old time's sake. Paul Gordon is the man she intends to marry and nothing can stop her. Okay. Grant all that. Would you mind telling me how all this is going to hurry up the marriage, or help you put over your Big Deal for Honeymoon House and the acres of land around it?"

Some sixth sense told her what Jerry was going to say before he said it. But it didn't warn her about the consuming fury that would possess her as she listened to his preposterous plan. "You're the one who will carry the ball from there on, honey."

He would arrange for Susan to come out to Carol's house before Bob arrived. That way the two girls could become friendly. She was to win Susan's confidence. By that time she should be on pretty good terms with Paul Gordon. As soon as Bob came, and Susan and he got together, in Carol's house, Carol was to get in touch with Paul and tell him, in strict confidence, what was happening.

"Pressure him into marrying Susan fast, before she has time to change her mind or do something silly with this lovesick boy who has followed her west. And naturally," Jerry finished, smiling, "that will mean buying the house fast. For he'll need a home to carry his beautiful little doll-bride into, won't he?"

Carol was shocked speechless for a moment. Jerry's scheme struck her as utterly absurd. But that was unimportant. What hit her with all the impact of a rock fired at her head was that Jerry should ask her to help him double-cross two nice people in order to make a few dollars.

He mistook her silence for consent. Coming over to her, his smile confident and winning, he ran his fingers through her silky dark hair, then with a casual gesture of affection bent his handsome head to smooth her cheek with his own.

77

"And don't forget this, honey. If we can put this deal over, including the acreage for the villa deal, it means I'll have it made. I'll be up in the big money class, and you'll go right along with me. We'll have a house that will be a show place. I'll buy you minks and diamonds and take you to New York and Paris to show you off. 'There goes Jerry Powers, one of the shrewdest financiers of our times,' people will say. 'And that's his wife with him.' "

He lifted her face and gave her a kiss. He was still smiling. "And when I introduce you, I'll say, 'Here's the little woman who helped me put it over. She made me what I am today.' How will you like that, sweetheart?"

All in one fluid movement she rose to her feet and her hand shot out. She struck him squarely across the cheek; then she did it again. "What's the idea?" Jerry asked, nursing his cheek as he stepped away from her. He looked more amazed than angry. "Have you gone out of your mind or something?"

She was breathing hard. "The idea is that I want no part of your cheap, childish, double-crossing scheme. If you think that I would permit that girl to use my home to entertain a friend, then go behind her back to make trouble with the man she's engaged to, you're the one who's out of *your* mind."

78

She stared at him for a moment, wondering why it had taken her so long to see Jerry for what he really was.

He was a man incapable of any real depth of emotion. That was the reason he had played fast and loose with her for so long. Incapable of an urgent, overpowering love for another person, he had no understanding of how deeply another person could be hurt. He was like a cold, greedy, superficial child. Money was his god. All other considerations were unimportant. He would meddle in the lives of Paul Gordon and Susan Starr gaily, even merrily, with never a thought for the somber truth that he might be destroying the happiness of two lives. In a way, she thought grimly, Jerry is a monster; a money-greedy monster.

The phone rang.

It was an excuse to move away from him. She couldn't bear to look at that handsome, lovable face, with no human understanding or sympathy behind it.

She crossed the room and picked up the receiver.

It was Paul Gordon explaining that he had been unavoidably detained. He'd be there in another fifteen minutes. "You'll wait for me, won't you?" he said.

She was tempted to refuse. Why should she wait? Paul Gordon meant nothing to her, or she to him. And as far as Jerry was concerned, there'd never be a better time to walk out and make him understand she was through.

"I'll wait," she said, and turned to Jerry who had come up behind her.

His face had sharpened, looked suddenly older, not nearly so handsome. He caught her arms, but not with affection. It was more a gesture of anger.

"All right," he said. "You don't have to say it again. I know what you're thinking. You've told me often enough that I'm obsessed about making money, and maybe I am. Well, it's easy enough to criticize the other person, my girl. But let me tell you something. There's an old Chinese saying: Never criticize the other fellow until you've walked in his shoes for three weeks."

He let go of her arms and started pacing the floor.

The phone rang.

"Don't answer it," he snapped. "Maybe if you had walked in my shoes when I was a kid, you'd understand better what makes me tick." His mouth was working, his face flushed under the tan. Carol had never seen him so worked up. What surprised her, shocked her vaguely, was that he was revealing things about himself he had never told her before.

She had known, of course, that his mother had died when he was born, his father a year later; and that he had been raised by an Aunt Bertha, an old maid who understood little or nothing about children.

But this was the first time he had ever gone into any details about Aunt Bertha's stinginess, her active dislike of him, the humiliations to which he had been subjected.

"The poorest kid in school had a little spending money," he said, "but not me. If little Jerry wanted so much as a nickel for candy, or to join in on something to which all the kids were contributing, Jerry was reminded that he was lucky to have food to put in his mouth, a bed to sleep in. What more did he expect?"

He walked back to Carol. His face came close to hers. He was staring at her, staring hard. Yet she had the curious feeling that he wasn't seeing her at all, was only dimly aware that she was standing there watching him, suddenly pitying him.

"It wasn't that she was poor. When she died, she left what she had to some relative back east. It was quite a tidy sum. But I was treated like a miserable piece of rubbish that had been wished on her. For some reason she hated me, maybe because she hated my mother. She was very religious. I guess that was the reason she took me in. She used to call it carrying the burden God had given her to carry. But she bought my clothes at

81

rummage sales; if I had to go to the dentist she took me to a free clinic. And when she went off on a trip, she'd leave me in the house with nothing to eat but stale bread and the kind of cheese you put in mouse traps." He said: "More than once the neighbors took me in and fed me, and bought me a clean shirt and a pair of decent shoes."

Suddenly he grabbed Carol's shoulders. "Now do you understand why I think money is the most important thing in the world? When I was no more than ten or eleven, I made up my mind that I'd be a rich man some day. If you haven't any money, you might as well be dead. You're nothing. If you have plenty of it, you're somebody and you can buy anything you want. That's what I decided. Now can you understand?"

There were tears in her eyes.

She put her arms around him, feeling warm and tender toward him, filled with pity. For a moment it was as if she were comforting an unhappy child. "Yes," she said low, "I understand now." She understood many things which she had never understood before. For one, why he seemed incapable of a deep, urgent love. It was because he had been denied love as a child, given coldness and cruelty instead. No wonder he had no deep love to give out. No wonder he had hurt her so often without realizing what he was doing to her.

"I can't help being the way I am," he muttered.

In a way, he was telling her he was sorry about the way he had used her to further his own plans, about the times he had hurt her, about the marriage plans that never came to anything. "I do love you," he said, "more than I've ever loved anyone."

Her sad little smile was hidden against his shoulder. Yes, she thought, that was probably true. She recalled the shy, reserved boy who had walked into her life when she was sixteen. She had given him coffee, cookies and her first deep love. Perhaps no one had given him any of those things before. Naturally he had responded. Naturally he had loved her, as much as he was capable of loving anyone. But that wasn't very much. That was the trouble.

"I'm glad you told me, Jerry," she said gently. "Now I understand you better." She held him close for a moment, but all she felt for him now was a great wealth of compassionate tenderness.

Her heart lay perfectly still.

After a time she walked away from him. Her smile was gentle. "I won't play any tricks for you," she said. "I won't mix into other people's lives or stir up trouble that might cause unhappiness. But I'll do anything I can to interest Paul Gordon in the house; anything I can do with a clear conscience, that is. Good enough?"

Jerry grinned at her. Having unburdened his soul, he was his charming self again. "Just put that sale over, honey. I'll play the tricks; you turn on the charm. That ought to do it."

Chapter Seven

From the moment she found herself behind the wheel of her car, with Paul Gordon seated beside her, Carol's nervous system began to play tricks on her. Fortunately she was an excellent driver, perfectly relaxed as far as handling the car was concerned, who had an unerring instinct for doing exactly the right thing at exacly the right split-second. This was an ability she could thank her lucky stars for. Otherwise the chances were good that both of them would have been dead, or at least serious emergency cases in the hospital, long before they reached Honeymoon House.

The trouble stemmed from tht vague, fluttery excitement she felt because of the way Paul kept watching her, studying her; and the way, every now and then, he would allow his hand to rest casually on her shoulder.

She could feel her pulse quicken, feel a warm flush mount her cheek. She had a bit of difficulty with her breathing, and once or twice her eyes refused to focus properly, with the result that she actually did drive against a red light signal.

Some character in a Continental car about a mile long shouted some extremely unpleasant remarks at her. A woman in a car the size of an over-sized bug shrilled: "Who gave you a permit to drive?"

"Would you mind taking your hand away from my shoulder?" Carol said coolly, turned her eyes, and found something definitely infuriating about the way Paul was grinning at her.

"Does it make you nervous to have me touch you?" he asked.

"Not at all. I simply don't like anything that takes my mind off my driving."

"Good enough. You concentrate on your driving while I concentrate on you. Has anyone ever told you that you have an extremely beautiful throat line? That's a rare thing, you know. If I were a sculptor, I'd go right to work on that lovely line."

"If it's all the same to you, would you mind cutting out your own line?" Her face was hot, her voice angry. It would have given her a great deal of pleasure to turn around and slap him—which made no sense at all.

She was silent, her eyes intent on her driving while her mind tried to figure out how this man could have a very definite attraction for her and at the same time arouse her antagonism.

"I wasn't handing you a line, Carol." He gave her a disarming smile. "Believe it or not, I wouldn't know how to go about handing a girl a line. Back in Texas where I come from, we just say what we think. If we don't think it, we don't say it. I truly do think you are a very beautiful girl, but if you don't want me to talk about it, I'll talk about something else. How about the California weather? That ought to be a safe enough topic."

They were leaving the heavy traffic behind, driving toward the hills back of Hollywood. Suddenly Carol felt ashamed of herself. I'm behaving like a petulant child, she thought. She turned and smiled at him.

"Please forgive me if I snapped at you for no good reason," she said. "I've had a rather hectic day. As a result, I seem to have mislaid my poise, as well as my common sense." She laughed. "Maybe I should start taking tranquilizers."

"Maybe you should find yourself a boy friend who appreciates you properly. Here was a guy lucky enough to have you willing to marry him, and he let you down at the last minute." Paul shook his head at the sheer stupidity of it, the folly of it. "The fellow sounds like a mental case to me."

This remark served to send Carol's anger whirling into high again. Her teeth bit into her underlip. She counted to twenty (ten wasn't enough) before she said coldly: "At some inconvenience to myself, Mr. Gordon, I'm driving you out to see a house in which you probably won't be interested. I shall point out all the beauties and wonders of it, because that's my job. I shall try to convince you that you'll be making the mistake of your life if you don't buy it. I shall also try to interest you in land around it which could make you another fortune in addition to the fortune you already have. When we get there, I plan to turn on the charm and give you a real honey of a sales talk. I'm not doing all this because I want to do it. I'm doing it because you insisted, and because it's an axiom in the Los Angeles real estate world: 'If you get hold of a sucker, don't let him get away from you.' In return, is it too much to ask that you keep your nose out of my personal affairs?"

This little speech was rewarded with a burst of hilarious laughter. Paul threw back his head and laughed and laughed until there were tears in his eyes. Finally he said, after calming down a bit: "Carol, honey, you're wonderful. You'd sure be fun to live with. There'd never be a dull moment with a smart gal like you around." He chuckled. "What a girl!" he said.

It was with a feeling of intense relief that Carol finally drove up in front of the pink, circular house which was built at the top of a sloping hillside.

"Well, here we are," she said, jamming on the brakes and turning to Paul with a cool, businesslike smile. I'll take him in and do my stuff, she thought. But so help me, if he makes any more cracks about Jerry and my misplaced affections, I'll turn around and walk right out. Let him find his way back to town alone. "You can see for yourself," she said sweetly, "it really does have a magnificent view. At night, when the lights come on, you can see all over Hollywood. It's like looking down at fairyland."

He grinned at her. "You're doing fine, honey." He got out of the car to follow her up the winding outside steps with the railing which looked like wrought iron but in fact was made of plastic.

Carol unlocked the door and led the way into an enormous room with a tiled floor and three walls of solid glass. "How do you open the windows?" was one of Paul's first questions.

"Don't be absurd." Carol smiled disdainfully at such an old-fashioned question. "This is the house of the future, my friend. Windows will be a thing

89

of the past. When you want fresh air, you step on a button. See? Like this." And she crossed the floor to where a series of tiny plastic-covered gadgets awaited the touch of a foot.

By mischance, however, Carol tapped the wrong one, and Paul gazed in amazement toward the ceiling as soft, dreamy music began to float down.

Carol burst out laughing. "Oh, Lord," she said, "walking into this house is like walking around on a crossword puzzle. One day when I was showing it and wanted music, what I got was the oven turned on full blast."

They stood for a moment listening to the music which, by some coincidence, was *The Dream of Love*. "You and your Susan can sit hand in hand, looking into each other's eyes, while that one is on," Carol said. "Won't that be nice and romantic?"

"Hm," Paul said, and lit a cigarette, whereupon Carol turned off the music, touched something else, and a plastic cigarette tray on a long flexible neck moved up out of the floor. Paul stared at it. Then he observed that this was the craziest house he had ever seen. Who had dreamed it up?

Carol observed that it probably wouldn't seem a bit unusual twenty or thirty years from now. It was just a matter of getting used to the idea that

90

electronics were being used in every phase of living.

"What we think of as wonders today will be commonplace tomorrow," she said. Jerry had been intrigued with the idea of building the "house of tomorrow" today. This place, she explained, was constructed almost entirely of plastic and glass. That certainly had its advantages. For one thing, plastic would never be favorite eating for termites, and termites were an absolute plague in southern California. They were everywhere. They ate into wooden beams; they got into the foundations of houses, even new ones. "And you wouldn't have any dry rot with plastic, either."

She took him into the kitchen, which was practically a museum of modern gadgets. She showed him the three bedrooms, the adjoining baths. Then she took him to the far end of the house into what looked for all the world like a miniature glass dome from a dome-liner train. "Here Susan can take her sun baths," she suggested pleasantly. "Or she might even use it for a hothouse to grow orchids, if you should happen to lose your millions, and couldn't afford to buy orchids for her," she said.

They looked at everything, and Carol explained everything—showed him all the wonderful, amazing conveniences of modern living. When he wanted to know where in heck a man could put some book shelves, she retorted: "Friend, how antiquated can you be! Book shelves! For what? In this brave, bright future that is coming up, who will want to read? For that matter, who will know *how* to read? If you want to know anything, Paul dear, you press a button. By the way, would you like to see the amazing colors of the sun rising over the Grand Canyon? If so, come hither."

They returned to the living room. She pressed a button. Dark plastic drapes closed across the walls, shutting out the sun and light. Another button, and the room swam in a pale, rosy glow which really did resemble the first eerie half-light of sunrise.

"Oh, turn it off," Paul said. "Let's have a little daylight. This house is weird. Got any chairs around a man can sit on? Without pushing a button, that is." He grinned.

Carol directed him to a closet. He came back with two straight-back chairs. Carol sat down. Paul straddled his chair, lit a cigarette, gave one to Carol and rested one arm on the chair back. "Now," he said, "do you honestly believe any normal, average man could live in this trick house without losing his mind?"

"I'm going to be perfectly honest with you, Paul. As to myself, no, I wouldn't care to live in this house. For that matter, I'm not in love with any of the modern homes. But then I suppose I'm about a hundred years behind the times."

She didn't, she said, care for so much glass, because she couldn't stand too much glare in a room where she was sitting. So for her, glass all over the place would simply mean buying yards and yards of expensive drape material to shut out the glare and hide the glass. What was more, she liked to read. Therefore, like himself, she liked book shelves, and wooden beamed ceilings, and an open fireplace. "But then I'm something of a freak." She smiled at him. "I wouldn't mind a bit living in a house built a century ago. I help sell these modern places. But I wouldn't want one for myself."

"How would you like living in a rambling Texas ranch house?"

"I'd adore it!" Carol said enthusiastically before she realized the implications of what she had blurted out. She laughed unconvincingly. "What I mean is, I think I'd like a ranch house anywhere, with a lot of quiet around. I simply hate noise. You get so much of it in a big city these days, what with motors racing and TV's blasting all around you and supersonic noises booming from the sky."

"Yeah. That's right."

They discussed city noises for some moments. It seemed a safe enough subject, one that worked an endless variety of comments and opinions. The only strange thing about the conversation was that Carol had the peculiar feeling that they weren't discussing noises at all.

Somehow their eyes seemed to get tangled up. Feeling self-conscious, she would tear her eyes away from his, only to look back and see that he hadn't taken his gaze off her. And it was such a strange, intent gaze.

If I didn't know better, she thought, I'd imagine he was making love to me with his eyes. The thought sent the blood racing wildly in her veins. She felt hot, she felt cold, she felt fluttery.

She got up suddenly. "Well, about this house: I've told you frankly what I don't like about it. I've leaned backwards trying to be honest with you. Now for the good side. I'm being equally honest when I tell you I'm sure it could be made into an absolute doll of a house."

"I don't doubt it," said Paul. He kept staring at her. Never in her life had Carol known a man to keep his eyes riveted on her face, as if she were a painting on a wall about which he was trying to make up his mind. It was embarrassing.

"Take this room, for instance. With a sweep of thick, white rug, and one of those huge semicircular divans, and maybe blue and gold fabric drapes, it could be heavenly. Actually, you can do wonders with any room. It's simply a matter of having good taste and plenty of money to spend. That's all."

"Yeah."

"And as for book shelves, I imagine something could be worked out. Anyway," she laughed nervously, "I doubt if your Susan is much of a reader, and she's the one to be pleased, isn't she?"

"Why do you keep referring to her as *my* Susan?" Paul inquired.

"She is your Susan, isn't she?"

"I wouldn't say so."

"But—"

"But what?" He got up and followed her to one of the expanses of glass, where she stood looking out toward the city. He stood close to her. She felt his hand on her arm. An amazing feeling of excitement quivered through her.

It had been a long, long time since the mere presence of an attractive man had excited her. She wasn't sure she had ever experienced quite such a feeling before. It set her to wondering about things that had never occurred to her before.

Had she ever been as wildly in love with Jerry as she had believed she was? Their relationship had been one of long, slow growth. She had been drawn to him when she was little more than a child, barely sixteen. It was the age when a girl was in love with love; was not mature enough or wise enough really to understand what deep, enduring love was, was not even ready for it.

Habit, she thought wonderingly. Maybe that was what it had been with Jerry, all that it had been. She thought, in a sense, holding fast to Jerry had been like keeping an old pair of shoes that were comfortable.

"Listen," Paul was saying. "You go ahead and decorate the house. Buy furniture. Figure out the right drapes and color schemes. Send the bills to me. But let's not bother talking any more about it."

"You're going to buy it?" She looked amazed.

"More than likely. You want to make the sale; it will get you in good with your boy friend, won't it? He may even be so pleased that he'll marry you as a reward for work well done." There was a hint of contempt in his tone, and a kind of anger, too.

Carol was blazingly angry again, but before she could think of a suitably cutting retort, he caught her arm and was practically forcing her toward the door and out of the house.

"I can't talk in this little curio shop," he said. "Let's go sit in the car. I want to talk to you about Susan. I want your advice."

"I never advise people about personal matters," Carol said icily. "What's more, if you're insinuating that you'd buy this house as a favor to me, just forget the the whole thing. This is a business

96

deal." In her fury her voice remained low, yet had all the impact of a scream. "I'm not asking for a handout."

"You're sure one attractive gal when you get your dander up," he told her. He was smiling again. "In fact, you're one attractive gal, period. Now come along, like a good little girl." And when she refused to budge an inch down the outside stairs, he simply hoisted her in his arms and carried her down.

Carol said the most childish thing she could possibly think of. "I hate you, Paul Gordon."

"Nonsense." He was laughing at her as he pushed her inside the car. "I have a hunch you're half in love with me. That's what makes you so snappy."

"I'm not snappy! It's simply that there's a certain type of remark I don't happen to care for when I'm doing business." That didn't seem altogether to cover what she meant, so she added: "Or even when I'm not doing business, if the man is way up on Cloud Nine over another girl."

His smile was enigmatic. "I was only kidding you, honey."

"I wish you'd stop calling me honey. And I can do nicely without your kidding, thank you." Her hands were clenched on the wheel. "I'll drive you back into town. Where would you like me to drop you off?"

"On the other hand, maybe I wasn't kidding. Maybe I sort of wish you *were* half in love with me, or even all the way in love. Heck, I don't even know what I do mean." He ran his hands worriedly through his thick reddish brown hair. The net result was that it stood up in a series of wild-looking spikes. His eyes, too, looked a bit wild, also worried. "You've got me all mixed up, Carol."

She turned to him, her smile several degrees below the freezing point. "You have every sign of a disturbed personality, my friend. Perhaps you should consult a psychiatrist. Now would you mind telling me where to let you off?"

He gave the question considerable thought before he said: "At your house. That's a good place to talk."

Chapter Eight

If there was one thing Carol was *not* going to do, it was to let Paul into her house again. She was beginning to wonder if he was a man who got romantic over every girl he met. He didn't seem that sort, but a girl never knew. In any case, he was simply a client. She had made it a rule never, for any reason whatever, to mix business with pleasure or to take a prospective buyer into her home. It could too easily lead to unpleasantness, or give a wrong impression about herself.

"Please, Carol." He argued about it. He begged. "Why shouldn't I go home with you? What's wrong with that? I come from Texas, where people are friendly and meet the other folks halfway. I'm lonely, honey. I'm out of place in this town. I haven't any friends here. I need to talk to somebody I can trust. I haven't anybody—except you."

"You poor darling!" Her eyes were filled with mockery as she swung the car onto the famous Strip. "My heart bleeds for you! Why didn't you tell me that Susan was deaf?"

"Oh, *Susan*." He sounded as if he were referring to a child still in kindergarten. He chuckled. "Susan is to look at, and buy things for, and pet. Sort of like a cute little kitten," he explained. She wasn't a girl with whom a man could sit down and talk about his worries and troubles. Anyway, he added, Susan was what he wanted to talk about.

"It wouldn't kill you to let me come in for an hour or so, would it? Don't be mean, honey."

Mean!

Somehow she found herself headed for Sierra Madre. She hadn't intended to give in, but what could she do? Three times in the downtown area she had stopped the car. "You could get a taxi from here," she had said.

No luck. Hollywood cab drivers bothered him, Paul said. They were safe enough drivers, no doubt. But they gave him a very pronounced feeling of insecurity. Even as he spoke, a yellow cab cut in front of Carol's car, missing her front fender by one sixteenth of an inch. "See what I mean?" Paul said, settling himself contentedly against the somewhat shabby red upholstery which would probably be in shreds before Carol could afford to buy a new car.

That was one of the thousand and one ways in which Jerry had never played altogether fair with her. No matter how much effort she put into making a sale, Jerry never cut her in on the profit. She was supposed to give her all for a relatively small salary—and love.

They were still some miles from Sierra Madre when Carol had to stop for gas.

Paul paid the attendant, then excused himself and went into a public phone booth at the side of the station. He returned, looking very thoughtful. "Your boy friend never misses an angle, does he?" he said, lighting a cigarette after he was back in the car.

"What do you mean?" Carol asked, as the car nosed into the traffic lane.

She was caught off guard by his next words.

He had phoned Susan, Paul explained. Early that morning, when he talked with her, Susan had been tucked away in bed nursing a serious virus cold she was afraid might develop into pneumonia. Not a chance that she would be up or in condition to see him for two or three days.

"She seems to have made a miraculous recovery." Paul's voice held no expression whatever. "It seems she's having dinner with Jerry Powers. Just

101

a little high-pressure work, no doubt." He looked hard at Carol. She could feel his eyes on her face, and when he asked the direct question: "Did you know about this arrangement?" she felt as guilty as if she's been caught snitching a cheap piece of jewelry from the Five and Ten.

"Jerry doesn't confide in me about everything he does." It was the most evasive answer she could think of without telling a direct lie. "Anyway," she rushed on, embroidering the evasion a bit, "what's wrong with his taking Susan to dinner?"

"I didn't say there was anything wrong with it. I merely asked if you knew that was the arrangement."

"As I just said, Jerry does all sorts of things he never mentions to me. He's forever taking some prospective buyer to dinner or lunch. That's part of Jerry's way of doing business. He's all for the personal touch. He'll probably buy Susan a wonderful meal," she added with the gayest of laughs, swerving the car into the outside lane to get around a slow, poky driver. "Jerry believes that a lot of good rich food puts any client in a more receptive mood for one of his sales talks."

She was talking too much, the way a person does to cover up something she wants to hide. She turned her face to him abruptly and caught him smiling at her with amusement.

"You're not a very good liar, Carol."

"I'm not lying!" she said hotly.

"Well, perhaps not. And for heaven's sake, honey, don't get your dander up again!"

"Then don't stare at me like that, as if you thought I weren't as bright as I should be."

"It's your boy friend who isn't any too bright. Or to put it another way, he's wasting his money on a dinner for Susan that isn't at all necessary. As I told you, I'll probably buy the house."

"Without knowing what Susan thinks about it?" she interrupted. "I thought that was the whole point: to find a house that Susan liked."

"That *was* the point, honey. But I've changed my mind. I've been thinking things over today. I've decided Susan doesn't know her own mind, so I'll have to make it up for her. If she wants me, she'll be happy in the house I buy for her. So I'm going to sign the contract for this one the day before Susan and I get married. I don't exactly go for this new-fangled, gadgety sort of place, but I think it should make a real nice present for any bride. Now what do you say about driving into that supermarket I see ahead and buying ourselves a couple of fine, thick steaks for our dinner?"

"Who said we were having dinner together?" Carol asked crossly.

"I said so, honey." He moved closer and swung his arm casually over the seat behind her. "Let's forget all about that house for the next few hours. Okay?"

When Carol said nothing, holding her eyes carefully on the highway ahead, he went on persuasively: "And there's another thing I'd like you to forget: that business about the phone this morning and me listening in to something that didn't concern me. You resent that, and I don't blame you. I'm very sorry about it, Carol. But don't hold it against me. Please don't. I think you're a sweet, charming, wonderful girl. You'd make a wonderful friend." All at once he sounded like a deeply troubled man. "And I need a friend, Carol. Have you ever wanted somebody you could talk to, talk over things that were bothering you; wanted it so bad that you actually ached? Have you?"

"Yes." Her tone was very gentle. How often, she thought sadly, how many, many times she had longed for somebody to whom she could pour out her heart. But from the day her beloved father had died, there had been no one. She had been too wrapped up in Jerry's life to make close friends. And Jerry wasn't the kind to give wise thought and understanding to the problems and inner conflicts of others. He was too wrapped up in himself.

"Yes, Paul." She repeated it, turning to him with warm, tender understanding in her eyes.

"I've wanted someone I could confide in. I know what you mean."

"Then will you take me home with you?"

I'd like to take you home with me forever, she thought.

She was suddenly afraid; afraid as she had never been before. Maybe it was not true that a girl could fall in love with a man at first sight, or even at second or third sight. Yet it had happened to her.

If, right then, Paul had offered her all the years of his life, she would have taken them, with joy in her heart and the wonderful knowledge that she was being taken home to the care and love of a man with whom she belonged.

But all he had to offer her was one little evening.

Her heart broke a little at the thought. It was so little.

Her forced smile was bright, her tone gay. "Let's go buy the steaks," she said.

Chapter Nine

"Now look what you made me do!"

It was one of those accidents which couldn't possibly happen unless you were terribly clumsy, unless you did it on purpose, or unless a man slipped his arm around you in a companionable way at the wrong moment, and made you so jittery that whatever you were holding slipped right out of your hand.

Carol had just drawn water into the double boiler to put on the stove. That was when Paul came up behind her; sneaked up and startled her, Carol insisted afterwards. She jumped, much as if she were connected with some electronic device which responded to the slightest touch—and the next thing she knew, the pan of water took on a life of its own.

It flew out of her hand, and a good quart of water went all over Paul's shirt and slacks. He was soaked.

"It was your own fault," Carol said.

"It's clear that you have all the makings of a nagging wife, honey." Paul gave her the most exasperating grin, fingering his dripping shirt. "No matter what happens, it will be friend husband's fault."

"Well, it *was* your fault. I never could stand having a man around the kitchen when I was fixing a meal, anyway. It never fails. But—" suddenly she burst out laughing— "I must say it's the first time I ever gave a man a shower bath in my kitchen. What are we going to do about you?"

Obviously he couldn't sit around with his clothes soaking wet. Neither could she send him on his way, after he'd spent a small fortune on the steaks which were waiting to go under the broiler. "I have a couple of over-sized towels," she said thoughtfully. "But you're such a big guy." So the towels would scarcely suffice.

"How about wrapping me up in a blanket while my slacks dry?"

Carol giggled. All of her blankets were of a soft baby-blue shade. "You'd look sweet in one of them, sort of like an over-sized baby." But no. A blanket would scarcely do.

Carol went into her bedroom and came back with an old woolen bathrobe she used in the winter. Except that the sleeves were a bit short and it reached only a few inches below his knees, the robe was perfectly adequate. "Couldn't be better," Paul said, when he came back from the bathroom where he had hung up his clothes to dry.

He couldn't think of more perfect attire for broiling steaks, which he insisted upon doing himself. He wanted Carol to see for herself, he said, what a fine cook and husband he'd make for any woman. "I'd be a real jewel," he said. "I don't suppose you'd be interested in kidnapping me, honey? I wouldn't put up a bit of fuss if you were to bind and gag me, then carry me off to some remote, far-away spot. Honestly I wouldn't."

"What makes you keep on saying such things?" Carol asked him.

It was later that evening. The beautiful steaks were now simply a beautiful memory. So was the fine red wine Paul had bought to go with them; and the asparagus tips, the French pastry, and the wonderfully good coffee, also brewed by Paul. The man could really cook, no question about that. The explanation was simple, he said. He lived by himself and did most of his own cooking.

On a Texas ranch there was no coffee shop handy around the corner. He was ten miles from the nearest town.

Now they sat on the divan drawn up before the open fire. Blue and yellow flames played over the eucalyptus log. Carol had on a turquoise blue housecoat. Her hair was tied back with a blue ribbon. She was smoking a cigarette with a last cup of coffee. "I know you better now, so I know that you kid a lot. And I sort of wish you wouldn't. I'm not sure it's very complimentary to me, and how do you think Susan would feel if she heard you suggesting running off with another girl, even in fun?"

"I'm not sure how she'd feel. That's my problem, Carol," he said, and for a full five minutes he didn't say another word.

He just sat there smoking his pipe and staring at the fire, his thoughts apparently a thousand miles away.

"That's why I want to talk to you about Susan," he said, what seemed about a year later. "You seem like such a wise, understanding person. And if I don't talk to somebody I'll go off my rocker!" These last words came with explosive force.

But instead of mentioning Susan, he started to tell her about a girl named Mary whom he had know a long, long time ago.

Mary Davis was her name; she was a dark-haired girl with a lovely smile. In the strict sense of the word, Mary was not beautiful. "But there was some inner quality about her that made her seem beautiful. Maybe it was a loving look. Know what I mean?"

"Yes." Carol nodded, reaching out her slipper-shod foot to rest it on the brass fender in front of the fire.

"She was a loving person. Mary loved everybody: children, old people, sick people, hurt people. Mary loved and was kind to all of them. In return, everybody loved Mary. I loved her. She was the only girl I ever loved seriously, or ever wanted for a wife."

"Didn't she love you, Paul?" Carol turned and caught the swift, deep look of pain in his eyes.

"Oh, yes," he said. Mary had loved him completely. The arrangements had all been made for their wedding, and for their life together. The ranch house was built. He had made most of the furniture with his own hands. He liked to work with wood. It was a form of recreation that gave him a lot of pleasure and satisfaction. So he had made all of the chairs for their house, and Mary had chosen the fabrics, done the upholstering. She had been good at working with her hands, too. That was one of the reasons they had been so sure their life together would be a really good life.

They were so much alike in their tastes, their interests, the things they liked to do.

"Then she was killed." He said it sharply, abruptly.

"Oh, Paul! What happened?"

He shrugged. "She was crazy about riding horses. It was her one outdoor sport. She was an excellent rider. She'd never fallen off a horse in her life. But she was thrown that day, and the horse went down on top of her. Her back was broken. She died the next day."

Except for the look in his eyes, Paul evinced little or no feeling as he talked about it. After all, it had all been a long time ago; eight years ago. He had been twenty-three at the time. He had gotten over his grief. Time had taken care of that. But as far as love was concerned, the lights went out on the day he stood outside of Mary's hospital room and the doctor came out, closing the door softly behind him, to give him the bad news.

"It's all over," the doctor had said, and for Paul the words meant that one phase of his life was over.

Mary was the woman he had wanted, and Mary was gone. So . . . Paul got up to tap out his pipe bowl over the flaming log. He turned and stood quietly, staring down at Carol, whose eyes were warm and tender and compassionate. She, too, was one of the ones who gave out warmth and love to all hurt creatures.

Perhaps it had been a mistake, Paul said, to turn into a kind of hermit. But that was precisely what he had done. He had moved into the ranch house with its reminders of the dreams he and Mary had once dreamed together. He had lived there alone. He had had plenty of work to do. There were cattle to look after, vegetables to grow. He planted and raised practically everything he ate. When he wasn't working, or playing poker with men companions in the evening, he had made a life out of reading, studying, tinkering at things around the house. He had built two extra rooms just to be doing something, to kill time.

Except for an occasional date which meant absolutely nothing to him, he had had nothing to do with women in all those years.

He came back to the divan, and a look of disgust spread over his face. "So I suppose I was ripe to make a fool of myself," he burst out, "or to have somebody make a fool of me."

Out of the blue he had inherited money which he honestly didn't want, from an uncle he hadn't seen half a dozen times in his life. That had brought him to Hollywood.

Want it or not, if you were suddenly informed that somebody had left you a fortune, you had to go see about it. Money was a responsibility. You had to look after a responsibility, didn't you?

Carol nodded. She said nothing. What was there to say? And she had the feeling that Paul was really talking things out with himself, rather than talking to her.

He took a long, deep breath, refilled his pipe, got it lit, and stared some more into the flames. "So I met Susan," he said, and he made it sound as if a serious calamity had befallen him.

Sighing, he shook his head. He hadn't gone dancing in so long that he'd forgotten how to dance. And he hadn't even kissed a pretty girl since he had lost Mary.

"It was like being hit over the head with an avalanche. I'm telling you the truth."

"You mean you fell that madly in love with her?" Carol asked.

No, he didn't mean that. He turned and looked at Carol, looked at her in that probing, thoughtful way she was beginning to get used to. It was as if he hoped to find the answer to a practically insoluble puzzle in her eyes.

"I haven't the slightest idea whether I'm in love with Susan or not," he said flatly.

"What?" Amazed, Carol stared back at him. "But you're engaged to her, Paul. You've showered her with expensive gifts. You—"

"Is it necessary to remind me of everything I already know?" he demanded, looking angry. "Sure. As I told you, she hit me hard. She is the most beautiful kid I've ever seen. Dancing with Susan is like dancing with a feather. Kissing her is like—well, you've seen the way it's done in the movies. Or to put it another way, for a few weeks I was like a man in a daze. I was so badly infatuated, I didn't know whether I was standing on my head or my feet. I was very sure the ground under my feet wasn't solid ground. I was stepping around on the clouds."

He paused to puff on his pipe.

"When I came out of the daze," he said, "I was engaged. I was committed to give up the life on my ranch which I love, to settle for a life here in Hollywood which doesn't strike me as any life at all. I was committed to marry a sweet little girl whom I wouldn't hurt for anything in this world. I—"

"Are you saying you don't want to marry Susan?" Carol asked. The log that was burning broke in half, and she got up to poke at it with an old piece of iron she had found one day on the beach.

When she turned back, Paul was standing close beside her. His eyes brushed her face. She felt as if his fingers, loving and gentle, were touching her. But he did not actually touch her. "I don't know whether I want to marry Susan or not," he said.

114

But that was not the question that was bothering him. After all, Susan was a nice person. As of now, she was little more than a beautiful child, a bit carried away by the consciousness of her own beauty. The beauty contest had turned her head, he imagined. But time would take care of that. Susan was bound to grow up, to grow older. She'd be a satisfactory wife, provided she was married to a man she loved.

"I'd be willing to chance it if I were sure she loved me," Paul said. "But—"

"You're afraid she's simply marrying you for your money," Carol said.

"I'm afraid her mother is pressuring her into marrying me for my money," Paul corrected her.

And then he said something that really rocked Carol! "I happen to know," Paul said, refilling his pipe for the third time, "that Susan was crazy about some lad back in Virginia. For all I know, maybe she still is. On the other hand, maybe this boy was simply a schoolgirl crush and she's all over it. If only there were some way I could get that lad out here," he said, "that might be the answer to everything."

While Carol was trying to decide what to say in reply to this amazing remark, she heard a car drive up outside. She glanced at her watch. It was close to midnight. Who could be coming to see her at that hour?

She heard footsteps on the flagstone path leading to her door, and she went to open it. "Hi, there, honey," Jerry said, his arm guiding the slender girl who walked beside him. "I've brought the prettiest little girl who ever came out of Virginia to meet you. Susan, this is Carol Kane. Isn't she a beautiful doll, Carol?"

Chapter Ten

And Paul was wrapped up in that silly bathrobe!

Carol thought with horror: If Susan finds him like that it could ruin everything.

Talk about embarrassing situations!

With a quick kick of her foot, Carol sent the screen door flying shut. "Hello, Susan," she said, and in the same breath: "I'm sorry I can't invite you in, but it doesn't happen to be convenient."

The moon was bright. It showed her the look of astonishment on Jerry's face as she gave him a determined push. He had been about to step up on her narrow concrete porch. Once she got him away from the porch, she caught his arm and pulled him back down the path toward his car.

Susan came tagging along behind. She was giggling. "I don't think she wants us to come in, Jerry," and she giggled some more. It was the uncontrollable laughter of a girl who had tasted champagne for the first time in her life and had drunk a little too much of it.

"What's wrong with you, Carol?"

They had come to the foot of the path, which seemed a fairly safe place to stand for a moment. It was almost twenty feet from the house. "Nothing is wrong with me, Jerry." And then she gave the flimsiest of all possible excuses.

She had, she said, just taken it into her head to clean the house. Everything was at sixes and sevens. The rugs were up; some of the chairs were upside down. "If you were going to bring Miss Starr out to see me, you should have phoned."

Then she took her first good look at Susan, who was sheathed in a black velvet dress which reached to her ankles. She had a box of crackerjack in her hand, and with the sweetest smile on earth she offered some to Carol. "I told Jerry it was too late to barge in on you," she said. "But men don't have a bit of sense about things like that, do they?" She had stopped giggling.

Carol smiled back at her and felt just a slight touch of envy. Susan's gorgeous hair was wrapped around her head in a fantastic, exaggerated fashion. On her it looked marvelous. She reminded

Carol a little of Audrey Hepburn. She really was a beauty.

"I don't get it," Jerry said, in the tone of a considerably puzzled man. He was studying Carol with deep suspicion. For the first time it struck Jerry that there might just possibly be another man in Carol's life. Since he had never thought of such a thing before, he was upset.

"You never before in your life cleaned house in the middle of the night." Carol got the impression he would have been less astonished had she said she'd been out robbing a bank. "I don't believe any such nonsense," he said.

"Are you calling me a liar?" Carol inquired pleasantly.

"Oh, Jerry! Don't be such a dope," Susan said, and produced another giggle. "It's obvious she has another boy friend, which is any girl's right."

"I'm going into the house," Jerry said. When he tried to push past her, Carol tensed with indignation. What had started as a ridiculous situation now seemed to her outrageous. What right had Jerry to come to her house at that hour, bringing with him a girl who was a stranger, and try to force his way in?

"You are not going in," she said emphatically, and stood squarely in front of him. "What my reasons are—well, that's really none of your business. This is my home, Jerry. And incidentally," she went on, her anger growing, "this happens to be the night when you and I were supposed to be in Palm Springs on our honeymoon. Remember?"

"What's that got to do with anything?" Jerry said.

"It's got everything to do with your coming here at midnight, as if you had the right to come whenever you felt like it. When you called the wedding off, you called everything off. You have no rights at all, Jerry—not any more." And then she turned to Susan with an apologetic smile.

"I'm sorry, Susan. I don't usually air my private grievances this way. I don't mean to be rude, either. If you and Jerry want to drive over to see me tomorrow, I'll be delighted to have you come. Okay?" She gave Susan a warm, friendly smile.

She might be slightly envious of Susan's beauty, but this was a nice kid. She didn't deserve to be hurt, and Carol would not be the one to hurt her. If Paul wasn't sure about his impending marriage, that was his problem. It wasn't up to her to walk Susan into the house and risk bringing on an unpleasant scene that might end their romance then and there. Let Paul make up his own mind and handle it in his own way.

Jerry had calmed down. He apologized. Okay, he said. It was stupid of him not to have phoned. Carol had every right not to invite them in if she didn't want to.

He slipped his arm around her, and she recognized all the signs of the wheedling, charming, loving Jerry who wanted her to do a favor for him. Jerry was always his sweetest when he wanted something. He was very sweet now as he hugged her close and said: "But Susan has a little problem, and we're depending on you to help us out."

"You'd better lower your voice, Jerry." Carol sent an uneasy glance toward the house. Susan's problem no doubt had to do with her Bob's trip to the coast. And how did she know that Paul was not standing by the window, listening to every word they said? Voices carried in the night when it was quiet. It was very quiet now.

"We don't konw but what some neighbor may be listening in."

So Jerry lowered his voice a bit. The problem had to do with Susan's Cousin Bob.

"He's the sweetest old thing, Cousin Bob is," Susan interrupted.

"Old?" Carol said.

Susan giggled. Well, not really old. That was just a way of talking in Virginia. As a matter of fact, Cousin Bob was still in his early twenties. And he had never been west. In fact, Cousin Bob had never been out of Virginia, and Susan had begun to worry that he might get lost if he landed in California with no one to meet him. Also, how would he ever communicate with her once he did get there? Oh, there had been ever so many details that couldn't be settled in a telegram. She had worried about it all day long.

"Couldn't Cousin Bob phone your apartment when he arrives?" Carol suggested.

"And chance having my mother answer the phone?" Heavens, no! That, said Susan, would be the ever living end.

"Susan's mother and Cousin Bob don't get along," Jerry reminded Carol. "I thought I told you."

"I forgot." Carol laughed. "This is all so complicated. It's hard to keep every little detail in mind."

"So anyway," Susan said, "this evening, while we were eating dinner, Jerry had the best little old idea. He suggested that I *phone* Cousin Bob, and *talk* with him, and get everything straightened out *that* way. So I did. And now I'm going to St. Louis. Isn't that exciting?"

"You're *what?*"

"I'm going to St. Louis. By plane. Early tomorrow morning. I'm going to meet Cousin Bob there, and we're flying back to California together. And what we want you to do is to phone my mother and say I'm spending the day and tomorrow night with you. We'll be taking the night plance back, see?"

While she talked Susan kept pushing popcorn

122

between her bright, pretty lips. She was as light-hearted about the whole thing as a thoughtless child; a beautiful, starry-eyed child who was planning a wonderful adventure. Apparently it didn't occur to her that she was planning a reckless, possibly dangerous undertaking, or that there was anything underhanded about what she was proposing.

Jerry was explaining the plan in more detail. "Susan plans to slip out of the apartment before her mother is awake. She'll leave a note on her pillow. The note will explain that I'm driving her out to look at that house, and that my partner, Miss Kane, is going with us. Then later in the day, say around noon, you're to phone and say you're taking Susan down to Laguna Beach for the afternoon. Say you have a little cottage there where you may spend the night. Okay?"

"Please say you'll do it, Carol!" Susan tucked a coaxing hand under Carol's arm. "Please? If you don't my mother might do some ridiculous thing, like calling the police."

Carol was uneasy, wondering if Paul, by any awful chance, was overhearing this conversation.

If only she were free to take them into the house, so that she could tell Jerry exactly what she thought of his irresponsible behavior.

Jerry needed telling off! This was a harebrained scheme, and Jerry was responsible for it. Instead of talking Susan into it, he should have talked her out of it. He was a mature man. Mad as he was to make money, to promote a business deal, surely it shouldn't have become such an obsession with him that he couldn't see the danger in Susan's proposed journey.

Suppose there was an accident?

Or suppose this charming child was led, or misled, into some reckless behavior on this trip with her Bob, about whom neither Jerry nor Carol knew the first thing. He might be the kind of man who would take the best of care of Susan. Possibly he would guard her as carefully as if she were his own sister.

But suppose he were just the opposite, and he took Susan's trip to meet him as a signal that she could be persuaded to do anything he might ask of her? And suppose Susan lost her head completely?

Oh, suppose any of a thousand things!

It was all wrong. Jerry should have had better sense. He was conducting himself like a schoolboy who was getting a kick out of helping promote the romance of two lovesick school kids. He was acting as if he'd lost his mind!

She wanted to tell them all that and a lot more.

But she couldn't.

Paul might be listening.

She spoke softly, but there was anger in her tone.

"I'm sorry, Susan, but I can't tell your mother any lies. If you want to deceive your mother, it's your own affair. But please don't ask me to help you deceive her. I can't do it."

"Now listen here, Carol." Jerry spoke irritably. "You don't have to sound off like somebody's maiden aunt. This is simply a case of a nice kid who wants to be free to have a day's fun. There's nothing wrong about it that I can see. Susan's mother is a problem, because she happens to be the kind of mother who wants to keep her little girl under lock and key. I'm all for giving this nice little girl one day to get out from under."

He was doing his part, Jerry said. He was going to drive Susan to the airport; he would meet the plane when she returned. "Why can't you help a little, honey?" he wheedled, and patted her arm. "Heck, you haven't forgotten what it's like to be young, have you?"

Carol softened, just a little. She could understand how it was with Susan. Quite possibly it was the sheer adventure of running away for a day that tempted her. But Carol was not going to lie for her!

"Well," said Susan, who had no intention of giving up her dreamy plan, "do you mind if *I* tell Mother in my note that I'm spending the day and night with you? She won't know how to reach you to ask any questions, so you won't have to say a word that isn't true. Will that be all right?"

"That will be fine," said Jerry, giving Carol no time to think it over or to reply before he pushed Susan into the car. "I'll get in touch with you in the morning, honey," he told Carol, and gunned the motor.

Carol went back into the house.

Paul, to all outward appearances, was sound asleep on the divan. He even produced a gentle, rather attractive little snore. Carol stood for a moment looking down at him. A dim suspicion flashed through her mind. How could he be as sound asleep as all that?

But no matter. Asleep or awake, he had to get up and get out of there.

"Wake up, you," she said as she leaned over to give her sleeping guest a vigorous shake. And when he opened his eyes, she sounded as firm as an aging school-teacher giving orders to an obstreperous pupil.

"I want you to get dressed and get out of here, fast. And don't ever come back. Is that clear?"

He sat up, rubbing his eyes sleepily. "Don't glower at me like that, honey." He reached for a cigarette. "What have I done wrong now?"

"Please don't call me honey. I'm not your honey. Your precious bit of honey was outside."

"With *your* sweetheart." After two or three

126

drags, he tossed the cigarette into the fire, which was still smoldering. "I heard them," Paul said. "What did they want?" He sounded very innocent. Carol wondered if it was an act. "Why didn't you bring them in?"

"With you in that silly bathrobe?" As for what they wanted, she explained: as Paul already knew, Jerry had taken Susan to dinner, then to a movie. That is, she believed they had said something about a movie. And after that, Jerry had had the brilliant idea of driving out to Carol's house. "He wanted Susan to meet me," she said lamely. It didn't sound very convincing, but what else could she say?

"And now I want you to go." She breathed deeply several times. "I mean it, Paul. I don't like to be placed in an embarrassing situation because of two people who don't know their own minds. And another thing—"

He stood up and caught hold of her arms. "Never mind all the explanations that explain nothing. There's just one thing I want to know. Why the sudden change in your attitude toward me?"

"I don't know what you mean."

"Oh, yes you do." His eyes raked her face. "I thought you liked me. I thought we were friends. I was beginning to dream that I'd found something very wonderful in your friendship. Everything was

127

going so well between us. Then *they* came. You went out to talk with them. You came back a changed girl. Why?"

She was silent, avoiding his eyes.

So he persisted, his hands tightening on her arms. "I want you to tell me why, Carol. Don't you like me? Is that it?"

She looked at him, then looked away again. She chewed her underlip, thought for a moment about the dazzling beauty of Susan, and decided on complete honesty.

Her head went up and her eyes looked straight into his.

"All right," she said. "You want to know, so I'm going to tell you. I'm afraid of liking you too well, Paul Gordon. I don't seem able to like a man in a casual way. I've wasted quite a few years being too intense over a man I now believe was all wrong for me. I loved him—or felt something that passed for love—and I got hurt. I don't want to get hurt again."

She was amazed at her own words. What had happened to her pride? How could she talk to him like this? But the words kept coming, as if they had an independent life of their own over which she had no control.

"I've seen Susan," she said finally. "She's sweet, she's young, she's altogether lovely." Her quick laugh was ragged. "And she's wearing your diamond ring. You're ready to buy a house for her. You'll marry her the day she says the word, and never mind all those doubts and uncertainties you mentioned. You'll marry her if she wants you to. Where do I fit into a picture like that?"

For a moment he simply stared at her with wondering eyes. Then, still without saying a word, he pulled her close. His mouth found hers, and for one little moment in time all Carol seemed to hear were her own thought waves beating out a desperate rhythm of words: If only he didn't belong to another girl.

Then she heard the wild pounding of her own heart. She wondered if he heard it, too. Or if he understood, even dimly, that she had never before experienced such a kiss. She was not sure that anyone had.

She drew away from him and pushed back her hair. Her heart was still fluttering like a wild thing, but her voice was cool and composed. "We'll just forget that happened, Paul."

"I'll remember it forever," he said softly. He cupped her flushed face between his hands. "And here's something for you to remember, Carol. I love you!"

"You have no right to say that!"

"Unfortunately it's true, darling. As for now, I have no right. Just the same, it's the way I feel about you." He held her close for a moment, his cheek warm against hers. "I've found my true love. I don't want to let you go."

With a sudden spurt of anger she drew away from him. "What you want is to eat your cake and have it too. You belong to Susan, and I don't want to get hurt. In the future, if you want to discuss anything concerning the house with me, you may phone me at the office. Now will you please go?"

"Sure, honey. I'll go." He was smiling as he headed for the bathroom and his drying clothes. "But as a very famous man once said, with any luck at all I shall return."

Chapter Eleven

Susan spent a restless night. She tossed and turned, twisted and pounded her pillow. She ground her teeth. Wide-eyed, she stared into the darkness. Right outside her window, a nightingale spent the night singing beseechingly to his mate. How could anybody sleep with a racket like that going on?

How could anybody sleep after the hectic day that she had had?

By sheer will power, she put Paul Gordon out of her thoughts, only to have him come stealing right back in again.

When she wasn't thinking about Paul and the strange, frightening hold he had taken on her emotions, she worried about Susan Starr and the way she, Carol, was becoming involved in the girl's heedless, unwise flight more than halfway across the continent.

Once she sat up in bed, turned on the light and reached for the phone. If she didn't want to be implicated in the affair, the thing to do was to call Susan, to tell Susan flatly not to bring her name into it. "If you do, Susan, and your mother should phone me, I'll have to tell her that you are not with me." That was certainly the thing to do. But—

Reluctantly she took her hand away from the phone without making the call.

She sat there thoughtful, leaning against her pillow. She was recalling something her father had said when she was fourteen or fifteen and they were discussing Cathy Baldwin, a friend of Carol's, whose mother tried to keep her a little recluse. Cathy's mother not only forbade all dates with boys, all dances, all pretty dresses; she didn't even want Cathy to have close girl friends.

As a result, Cathy was forever dreaming up fibs in order to get out of the house and have a little fun. Several times she had asked Carol to back her up in her flimsy stories, and Carol had asked her father about it.

"Cathy wants me to say she's been at my house, if her mother should ask me. What should I do, Daddy? I feel so sorry for Cathy. It's absolutely horrible, the way her mother won't let her do anything. But I don't like the idea of lying."

Professor Kane had thought for a long time before he replied, and even then what he said had been a bit ambiguous.

"There are lies, and there are lies," was the way he had put it. "Generally speaking, Carol, I hate a liar. It usually denotes a lack of character. But as with everything, there are exceptions. There are times when a young person is forced to find some means of defense against an overly domineering parent who refuses allow her the freedom every living thing is entitled to. Your friend Cathy is a fine, good, high-spirited girl. Unconsciously, she is fighting to be allowed to develop her individuality, to make her own decisions and to live her own life, as eventually she must do. In a sense, Cathy is fighting for survival. I suspect that is what Cathy's sad little lies are all about."

And then he had said, with his gentle smile: "The birds have more wisdom than many humans. As soon as the little ones are able to fly, the mother bird pushes them out of the nest and tells them to get going."

He never did tell me to back up Cathy in her stories, she thought now. But he certainly didn't tell me not to. So maybe he had simply been advising her, as he often did, "You have to make your own decision, Carol. It's for you to determine what's right or wrong."

She turned out the light and tried again to sleep.

It was around ten in the morning when Jerry phoned her. He was in fine spirits. Everything was going beautifully, he said. He had seen Susan off on the plane. It was a jet, and was the kid ever thrilled!

"By the way," he said laughingly, "Cousin Bob is her school sweetie, all right. We had champagne for dinner. After half a glass, Susan opened up and told me all about Bob. It seems he wrote her, begging to see her just one more time before she married. So that's what it's all about."

Well, that was that. If Susan was on her way, there was nothing Carol could do about it. No use wasting words giving Jerry another lecture. He would simply laugh at her. It wouldn't change anything. "What about that note she was going to leave for her mother, Jerry? Did she drag my name into it?"

For once Jerry was vague. "The kid was too excited before she took off to mention any details, honey." But if by any unlikely chance Carol should receive a phone call from Mrs. Starr: "You be very careful what you say, see? For heaven's sake, don't let on that Susan isn't with you. You'd ruin everything if you gave her away."

"What do you mean: I'd ruin everything, Jerry? The worst that could happen would be that Susan would be in for an ugly quarrel with her mother when she returns." She gave a mirthless laugh. "I should think this reunion with her old boy friend would be worth a heated lecture from her ma."

"Ruin everything for me!" Jerry said, speaking with considerable heat himself. Ruin the sale of the house.

"Listen to me, sweetheart. As of right now, I have little Miss Apple Blossoms eating out of my hand. *I* dreamed up this idea of a St. Louis trip."

"Oh, you did! Well, it sounds like you, Jerry." Her voice was cutting. "Had it served your purpose, I suppose you'd have sent Susan off to the Congo."

"So I'm really her boy," Jerry went on, ignoring Carol's sarcasm. "She figures I'm Santa Claus in a Cadillac, and you know how eager kids are to keep in good with Santa Claus. So I made this little deal with her."

"What little deal, Jerry?"

He chuckled. "I engineered the trip and promised that you and I would back up her story to her mother. In return, she promised she'd put the pressure on Paul Gordon to sign the contract for Honeymoon House as soon as she got back. See how things work out when you play all the angles, honey?"

"Maybe you're playing all the angles," Carol said coldly. "Then again, it just could be that you're playing with dynamite." And she hung up.

She spent the rest of the morning doing the vigorous cleaning which she had pretended to be doing the night before. It was a way of working off energy, of calming herself.

She ran the vacuum cleaner, she cleaned and polished several brass pieces. She waxed the nest of mahogany tables which she had had the luck to buy cheap in an antique shop, and all the time she was working she kept wondering about Susan Starr's trip. She was not superstitious, did not believe in psychic premonitions, and yet she could not throw off the uneasy feeling that something would go wrong before Susan got back.

Oh, stop worrying about it, she ordered herself. You had nothing to do with it; it isn't your responsibility. If that beautiful child should get herself in some sort of a jam, it would be too bad—but you had nothing to do with her taking off on a jet plane. The chances are that nothing will happen, except that her mother might phone you. And if she does, simply tell her . . . what?

Before she worked out the answer to that question in her own mind, the phone did ring. When she heard Paul Gordon's voice, asking if Susan was there, she was shocked speechless.

This was the one contingency she hadn't

thought of, and for a minute all she could do was wonder why she hadn't had the foresight to lock up the house and go somewhere for the day. Now she was trapped.

"I just had a phone call from Susan's mother." Paul sounded curt, anything but friendly. "She tells me that Susan has disappeared, leaving a note saying she was spending the day and night with you. I promised I'd get in touch with you and check up."

After an interminable time, Carol found her voice. "This is a little hard to explain," she said carefully. "Susan has been having a rather difficult time with her mother, and she's sort of nervous and upset."

"What seems to be the trouble, Carol? I mean, exactly what is she so nervous and upset about? Choosing a house? Getting married?" He spoke pleasantly enough, but Carol had the miserable feeling that he was simply probing to see what she'd say, that no matter what she said he wouldn't believe her. Paul was no fool.

"Oh, you know how young girls are," she said vaguely. "They get emotionally upset for no particular reason. No, I wouldn't say that the house, or getting married has a thing to do with it. It's just that she wanted to get off by herself for a little while. She said she felt as if she'd fly out of her skin if she couldn't get away from her mother for a day and a night." She gave an unconvincing laugh. "Anyway, she asked me if I'd help her out. That was the reason Jerry brought her here last night, so she could talk it over with me."

"I see," Paul said, in the tone of a man who saw nothing except that he was being given a lot of evasive talk. "You and Susan seem to have become fast friends last night. Remarkable," he commented after a brief pause. "She couldn't have been there more than ten minutes."

"Oh, longer than that, I'm sure."

"Well, let's say twenty minutes. Carol, why are you lying to me?"

"I'm not!" As a matter of fact, she thought, I haven't said a word that isn't true—more or less.

"All right," Paul said. "If you aren't lying, then please let me talk with Susan."

"I can't."

"Why can't you? I simply want to hear her voice so I can report back to her mother. She does happen to be my fiancée, you know. I shouldn't think it would interfere too much with her day of glorious freedom to say hello to me." He couldn't have sounded more sarcastic or more skeptical.

"She isn't here at the moment." That was certainly true enough.

"And she hasn't been there! Why are you covering up for her, Carol? What are you trying to hide?" His voice had softened just a trifle. There was a touch of desperate pleading in it, as if he were begging her to straighten out for him something that really had nothing to do with Susan. "Listen, Carol, if Susan is simply trying to put something over on her mother, why can't you tell me about it? I'd understand. I'd even help her. I simply want to be assured in my own mind that Susan is okay. This whole thing seems a bit mysterious, and it bothers me."

"Oh, don't let it bother you," Carol said airily. "You've read Susan's note, which explained everything. And I've told you that she's perfectly okay. She simply wanted to fly the coop for a day, that's all."

"No, that isn't all." Suddenly he sounded quietly furious. "There's a lot more to this than you're telling me. I have a very strong hunch that your friend Jerry Powers is mixed up in it somehow. Whatever you're hiding, or trying to hide, you're doing it for that man who's used you for years to pull his chestnuts out of the fire."

"How dare you say a thing like that to me, Paul Gordon?"

"I'm simply quoting your own words, lady. They were practically the first words you ever said to me. Remember? And I'll tell you something else!" The anger in his voice was growing, deepening. "I wasn't asleep last night. I didn't try to hear what was being said, but I couldn't help hearing

139

some of it. Your friend, Jerry, has a carrying voice. I know there was something he was trying to pressure you into doing, and it concerned Susan. You kept saying, 'I won't,' but in the end you gave in. You always give in when he asks you to do him some favor. Don't you?"

"Now you listen to me, Paul—"

"No. You listen. I'm doing the talking, and never mind what Susan is up to. Probably it's nothing too serious. Anyway, I hope not. What hurts me—and believe me, it really hurts—is that I'd been building you up in my mind as a girl who was completely honest in every sense of the word. After I left you last night, I walked for two or three hours just thinking about you. I had the feeling that you were the girl I'd been waiting for ever since I lost Mary. Susan was a mistake. I was forced to face it. All I could do about that was hope that something would free me from Susan without my having to let her down or hurt her. Then I thought I'd come straight to you. You see," he said, and for the first time in her life Carol wondered if she were hearing a man sob over the phone, "I believed what you said about caring too much for me."

"It was true," she murmured, close to tears herself.

If he heard her, he gave no sign.

"I believed every word of it. I lived on those

140

words for hours! I said them over and over to my-self. They seemed the sweetest words anyone had ever said to me; the truest! And they were a lie."

"Paul, please—"

"Don't talk to me. You were simply staging a dramatic act to get me out of the house and keep me out. You cared too much to have me come back, you might get hurt. Yeah! What you care about, all that you care about, is helping your boy friend put over some tricky little scheme to further his own ends."

"You don't know what you're talking about, Paul Gordon!"

"I know that. I haven't the vaguest idea what he's roping Susan into or why he's doing it. But I know something strange is going on. He's up to something, and you're backing him up in it. Susan isn't with you, and she never has been, except for a few minutes last night. You'd do anything that guy asked you to do. You'd lie for him until the cows come home. And I was fool enough to be-lieve there was something good between you and me. What a sap that makes of me!"

He sounded as if his heart were breaking. But before Carol had time to decide if it was simply her imagination, or to think what she could possi-bly say in her own defense, she heard his short, harsh laugh. Then the connection was broken, and she sat there on the bed with the receiver still in her hand, staring at nothing.

Well, she thought finally, that dream didn't last long. Her eyes blurred with tears. Her heart felt sick with despair. She thought, he walked around all night thinking about me. And now . . . she threw herself down on the bed and let the sobs come.

She had never before known how much love could hurt.

Chapter Twelve

Susan leaned her arm on the restaurant table by the window and stared out at the rain which had been pouring down on St. Louis all day long.

"Everything went wrong, didn't it?" She turned away from the dismal downpour to smile sadly at the slight, red-haired young man who was gazing lovingly at her. "We couldn't even sit in the park and hold hands. Oh, Bob!" It was a heartbroken little cry as she reached for his hand, which came to meet hers across the table.

They sat and looked at each other while the soup which neither of them wanted grew cold.

"And I thought it was going to be so wonderful." Susan sighed bleakly. "I thought we'd cram a lifetime of living into a few hours. Instead we haven't had anything at all."

"We've had two hours together, honey," Bob Connor said. "We've seen each other. And we'll have the trip back to California. After that—"

"Oh, sure. After that—" She took a sip of water, pounded at the table with a savage little fist, and renewed the argument which had begun almost as soon as Bob had stepped off his plane, six hours behind schedule.

That was the first thing that had gone wrong. The flight of the plane Bob had planned to take had been canceled at the last minute. It had been mid-afternoon before he had crossed the landing field to take Susan into his arms.

Half crazy by that time with worry and impatience, Susan had clung to him in sobbing desperation. Almost the first thing she had said was: "I thought that there'd been an accident and you were dead. I wanted to die, too. And I made up my mind if you turned up alive, I'd never let you go. I won't marry anybody else, darling. *I just won't do it.*"

Bob had refused to discuss the matter at the moment, other than to say he'd better make sure about their reservations on the plane to California that night. With Susan pulling at his arm, begging him to forget about California planes, fighting him every inch of the way, Bob went to take care of their tickets. He gave their names so they would be on the scheduled passengers' list.

Then he told Susan: "I agreed to let you meet me here, baby. I did not agree to botch up your life for you."

"You think marrying you would be botching up my life?" She gave him the look of a girl who was geared for battle. "Bob Connor, how stupid can you be?"

"Pretty stupid, I'm afraid. Anyway, terribly weak where you're concerned," he said, taking her arm to walk her out to where the bus going to the city was parked. "If I weren't, I wouldn't have let you take a chance on this trip. But I'm not stupid or weak enough to let you throw away your life by marrying the wrong guy."

"You're not the wrong guy! I found out whom I wanted when I thought maybe you'd been killed. I nearly lost my mind." She clung frantically to his arm, raised her streaming eyes to his. "*You* the wrong guy! How can you say a thing like that, Bob?"

"Because I love you enough to say it, honey. I'm just a small town boy who's never had very much and probably never will have much. I'd like to give you the moon, baby, but I know I'll never be able to. I'm just not the type. So the best I can do is hand you over to the millionaire who can give it to you. Now let's not spoil the few hours we have left arguing about it."

"You don't love me or you couldn't talk like that!"

"I love you, sweetheart, but I'm not for you."

So little time was left!

Not even time enough to go to a show, to bask in the comfort of sitting close in a darkened theatre. No time to wait for the rain to stop, so that they could wander the street arm in arm and pause to gaze into shop windows, aware of nothing that they looked at because they were aware only of each other.

No time, no time, no time for anything except to take a cab to the dreary old railroad station where they sat sadly, watching the people go by, watching the clock racing madly around, swift, uncaring, as it snatched the precious moments away from them.

"Well, honey," Bob said finally, "I guess we'd better go hunt some chow. We've got to eat, you know."

"Why?" said Susan, who did not care if she never ate another bite of food.

So now they sat in the small restaurant, and Susan said again the thing she had been saying at regular intervals from the moment she tore her lips away from Bob's, after his kiss of greeting. "There isn't a reason in this world why we shouldn't get married. Honestly there isn't. Right away, I mean. I'll send Mother a wire afterwards. She'll blow her top, of course. But she'll get over it, and as for Paul—" She pushed at her hair, looking thoughtful. "Well, maybe it would be a mean trick to play on him, but it wouldn't be half as mean as marrying him when I don't want to. Would it?"

Bob smiled at her. "That's a mighty pretty ring, honey," he said, touching the blazing diamond on her engagement finger. "It must have cost more than I'm likely to make in the next five years as a lawyer."

"All you think about is money," Susan said crossly, only to have Bob deny that emphatically.

"You're dead wrong about that, honey lamb. All I'm thinking about is you." Right then the thirtyish, weary-looking waitress spilled a little water over Susan's sleeve as she went to refill the glass.

She was terribly apologetic. "I don't half know what I'm about," she said in a voice that sounded weak with nervous tension. "I've been on my feet since ten o'clock this morning. My feet are killing me, and I feel like I'm coming down with virus flu, like most everybody else. With all the germs you breathe in a place like this, how could a body help catching something?"

"Why don't you go home and go to bed?" Susan asked sympathetically. "My goodness, I don't think it's right to make yourself go on working when you feel so awful."

"Because I need this job, that's why I don't go home. They're short of help here. Two girls walked out this morning without giving notice, and the boss is boiling. He'll take it out on the first girl who wants to quit ahead of time."

The waitress was the kind who was only too ready to air her grievances against germs, the boss, and life in general. For reasons best known to himself, Bob deliberately encouraged her.

"Suppose he did fire you, miss?" he inquired pleasantly. "Do you need this job that badly?"

"Do I need this job, mister!" Hands went to her hips; her laugh had a hollow sound. "With a husband out of work half the time and three little kids with great big appetites? Do I need this job bad! Prices keep going up, up, up, and everybody's out to rob you, right and left. There's not a thing poor folks can do about it except to keep working. You bet I need this job, mister."

As she turned toward another table, Bob stopped her with another question. "If it isn't too personal a question, what does your husband do, miss?"

"He's a plumber."

Susan chimed in, "Well, my goodness, if he's a plumber, I should think he'd make pots of money."

148

"You think that, huh?" The woman cast a plainly envious glance at Susan's blazing diamond. "Well, you listen to me, sister; you've got a lot to learn. I bet it wasn't any plumber gave you that pretty ring you're wearing."

Susan laughed her pretty laugh. "No, that's right, although the man who gave it to me can do plumbing if he has to. He told me once that if he ever went broke, he thought he might go into the plumbing business because of all the money plumbers make. Why, out in California where I come from, we had to pay a plumber six dollars to open a drain pipe, and he wasn't in the place five minutes! I think six dollars is pretty good pay for five minutes work, I don't care what anybody says."

"Yeah. Sure. I agree with you about that." The woman shifted her weight from one foot to the other. "But it's like I said to Fred the other day. He was griping because he hadn't had any work for close to two weeks, and us with I don't know how many bills to pay. I said to him, 'Fred, you lousy bums have priced yourselves right out of work, and you ain't got sense enough to know it. People will learn how to fix their own plumbing, and then what will you do?"

She gave a short, grim laugh. "You want to know what Fred said?"

Bob was interested. "I imagine he told you to

stop worrying," he said with a smile; "that he was an able-bodied man who could always get a job. Was that it?"

"A lot you know, mister. My Fred said: why should he worry? I was a good waitress, wasn't I? What with my salary and tips, I made pretty good money, didn't I? So with me to support the family if he couldn't, why should he sit up nights chewing his nails and shortening his life?"

"Jeepers!" Susan burst out, looking slightly amazed. "What a funny way for a man to talk."

"You think so, miss? Well, let me tell you a thing or two. That's the way plenty of them talk these days. They fight and fight to get their pay raised, until finally they haven't got any work or pay to speak of. Then they sit back and let the little woman take over." The waitress sounded downright vehement as she added: "A lot of men these days are turning into bums. That's what it gets down to."

"Well, there you are, honey," Bob said.

"What do you mean: there I am?" She gave him a belligerent look. "I suppose you think all that yakking backs you up, and that now I'm convinced I ought to marry for money."

"I didn't say you should marry for money, baby. What I do say is: if you can marry a man who is good and kind, a man you can like and re-

150

spect, and he happens to be in a position to keep you like a queen in addition—"

"I don't want to be kept like a queen. What I want is to be kept by you, and I wouldn't care if I did have to go to work. Lots of women work, so why shouldn't I? Anyway, you aren't a plumber. You're going to be a lawyer."

"Maybe, one of these days. Do you know what statistics show about the average income of the average lawyer?"

Her eyes blazed. "What do I care about statistics, Bob Connor. My heart is breaking, and you want to talk about statistics."

He tasted his coffee, lit a cigarette and leaned toward her. "Statistics show that a plumber has a larger income, on the average, than a struggling young lawyer."

Susan sighed deeply. "You heard what the woman said, Bob. This plumber husband of hers is out of work half the time."

Bob grinned at her. "Plenty of lawyers are out of work nine tenths of the time." He caught her hands, suddenly became deadly serious. "You're tearing us both to pieces talking about it, Susan. Please stop. I can't break up something I believe is good and right for you. Don't ask me to. Have a little pity. Have you any idea how hard you're making it for me?"

"In other words, you won't marry me."

"That's right, honey." He smiled a painful smile. "The gentleman begs to be excused."

"So this is all we're to have—just these few hours that turned out all wrong." Her eyes were shining with tears. "I'll probably be sick on the plane; I always am. So that won't be any good, either. Once we get to Hollywood, I don't even know how or where I'll manage to see you alone. Out there everything will be so complicated."

"No, it won't," he said very gently. He held her hand captured in both of his. "It won't be a bit complicated, because once we're there, I'm not going to see you." He shook his head. "There's no use going on torturing ourselves, Susan. I don't even want to see you out there. Every time it would be the same kind of punishment; a reminder of what I'm losing."

She snatched her hand from his, and her mouth fell open in astonishment. "Do you mean to sit there and tell me we aren't ever going to see each other again, once we're in California. Are you serious?"

"I was never more serious in my life, baby."

"Well," she said, "that really does it." And for a full five minutes she concentrated on eating the ice cream which she did not know she was eating, and smoking a cigarette which left a bitter taste which she never noticed. She didn't say a word, wouldn't even look at Bob.

"Excuse me for a minute," she said suddenly, crumpling her paper napkin and getting up from the table. "I just thought of something I have to attend to."

When he asked her what she was up to, she told him sweetly: "I'm going to phone my Aunt Clara, Sweetie Pie."

He thought she was making a joke.

But he couldn't have been more wrong.

Chapter Thirteen

It was nearly twenty minutes before Susan came tripping back to the table. She was all smiles now, her expression that of a triumphant cat who had just swallowed the canary, as she called their waitress friend and asked for a cut of apple pie heaped with ice cream and more coffee. "I'm suddenly ravenous," she informed Bob, who was dimly disturbed by the abrupt transformation.

"This is the first time in days," she said, "that I've had the faintest interest in eating. Now—" laughing gleefuly, she sipped water—"I feel as if I could gobble up every single thing on that steam table. And stop scowling at your watch, Bob honey."

"We have a plane to catch, Susan."

"No." She shook her head vigorously, thanked the waitress for bringing her such a beautiful, luscious-looking piece of pie, and announced to Bob that they were spending the night with her Aunt Clara.

"You remember Aunt Clara, don't you?"

"I can't say I do, honey."

His eyes were troubled, half-sick with love of her, and at the same time very suspicious. In fact, his eyes were telling her, I'm very sure you haven't got any Aunt Clara. I'm very sure this is some kind of a trick to get your own way. Why, my darling, must you make things so hard for me? You know how I love you, always have, always will. Don't you know how it makes me feel when I sit here looking at your beautiful face, know that it is engraved on my memory for all time, but know, too, that it is for some other man to look at through all the years to come.

How do you think it makes me feel when I sit here and think that *he* is the one who will be with you through all the happiness and joy and trouble and sorrow in the years ahead? *He* is the one who will laugh with you, comfort you when you are sad, care for you when you are sick. *He* will watch you grow old, grow old with you. He is the one to whom you will seem even more beautiful years from now than you do today, because he will have shared so much living with you and the age lines in your face will be tender reminders of all you have been through together.

Don't you know how it tears me apart to think about all this? Don't you know that what I want more than anything on this earth is to marry you and keep you for myself, always?

And don't you know, by giving you up, I am giving you the final proof of how greatly I do love you? Oh, Susan, surely you must know! I don't have to tell you in words. So why do you have to make things harder than they already are?

"I'm positive you never had an Aunt Clara, and if you're simply dreaming up a scheme to prevent us from getting on that plane—"

But Susan insisted that she did have an Aunt Clara. "I guess you knew her as Aunt Jess, Bob." Jess was her first name, and that was what the family back home always called her. But after she married again and moved to St. Louis, she decided she preferred to be called Clara, which was her middle name. Her second husband was rather prominent in politics. His name got in the papers quite a lot, and his wife's name, too, and he didn't altogether like the sound of Jess Johnson for publicity purposes. "It offended his sensibilities, Aunt Clara says," Susan explained.

Okay. Grinning, Bob accepted the somewhat confusing explanation. He remembered Aunt Jess. She was the only one in Susan's family who had ever been really friendly to him. "I hope you remembered me to her," he said.

He gave another worried glance at his watch. The fact remained that time was flying. They had less than an hour to get to the airport. With the rain pouring down in torrents, it might take a little while to get a cab.

"How often do I have to tell you, Bob Connor? We are not getting on that plane, so we won't need any cab. We are going out to Aunt Clara's. She says she'd be mortally offended if we didn't come. She just couldn't imagine my being in this city and not coming to spend a few days with her. She'd be hurt, Bob, honestly."

And if Bob thought for one minute that she'd offend dear Aunt Clara, he'd better think again. Aunt Clara had always been closer to her than her own mother. Aunt Clara had been the one who was always calling her mother to account for being too domineering and too possessive. "Once she told Mother that she'd ruin my life if she didn't stop trying practically to tell me how to breathe!"

Whenever there was an argument between Susan and her mother, Aunt Clara was always on Susan's side. A girl would have to be pretty ungrateful not to appreciate that kind of an aunt, and not to want to pay her a visit when she was passing through St. Louis.

"And she has this great big house, with I don't know how many guest rooms," Susan told him, coming at long last to the real details. "She's absolutely mad with joy at the thought of having you and me stay with her for a few days. And she's coming in her car to get us, so why don't you relax, Bob? Order some more coffee for yourself. Smoke some cigarettes. We have time to burn."

She had finished the pie and ice cream. This gave her time to observe Bob more closely. He was scowling at her! And at the same time his eyes looked terribly sad. You'd have thought she'd just said she was going to abandon him in the snow, or something. He was certainly acting strangely.

"We can't do it, Susan." He was saying it as if he actually meant it. "For one thing, your mother doesn't know where you are. You'll have a hard enough time explaining when you get back tomorrow. How do you expect to explain being gone for three or four days?"

She gave him an airy smile. "I won't have to. Aunt Clara will do the explaining for me. On the day we leave, she says she'll phone Mother long distance and say that I've been visiting with her. She won't have to mention your name."

"I see. And how will you explain being in St. Louis to start with? And what's more to the point, what will you tell Paul Gordon?"

Bob crushed out the cigarette he had been

smoking. His eyes looked sadder than ever as he stared at her, but his mouth was set in a stern, tight line. He wouldn't listen to any more of her explanations and pleas. He said she was just trying to make him forget that time was passing, while she wheedled to get her own way. And if he were to give in and go to Aunt Clara's, he would have to endure more of the same.

"You'd probably spend the whole time trying to talk me into marrying you against my better judgment." His hand was clenched, his jaw firm. "And if I gave in on that, a year from now you'd probably hate the sight of me! For every time you looked at me, and looked at the cheap little apartment which would be the best I could afford, you'd be thinking of the easy, beautiful, glamorous life you might have had if you hadn't been fool enough to marry me. Now come along!"

He got up, leaving money on the table to take care of the check and a tip. When Susan refused to budge, he walked out of the restaurant alone.

He waited outside.

When she came, after a moment, she was crying. She refused to speak to him. When a cab stopped at the curb, she got into it ahead of him. But she still refused to speak, no matter what he said. When he tried to put his arm around her, she slapped him. And all the time tears were spilling gently from her eyes, making glistening beads over her flushed cheeks. The driver headed for the airport.

The rain kept pouring down.

Susan turned her face away from Bob, staring out at the rain, at the people hurrying to get out of it, at the city. Everything looked so dreary, so sad.

Suddenly Susan leaned forward and told the driver: "Please stop right here. I'm getting out." And before Bob could stop her, she was on the sidewalk, walking away in the drenching rain.

He paid the driver and hurried after her. He caught her arm. "Susan, honey, please! You can't do this."

She kept on going, head bent against the rain, her body tensed against his effort to shield her a little with his arm. "Don't touch me," she said thickly. "Don't talk to me. Why don't you go get on that plane? I wouldn't have you miss it on my account."

"Susan, I love you. Can't you understand that? I'm trying to do what's right and good for you because I love you."

"And I'm sick and tired of people who want to decide what's right and good for me, and pretend it's because they love me so much."

Suddenly she stopped and raised her wet face to his. "That's what my mother has been doing my whole life long: making me do things I didn't want to do because it was good for me. *She* knew

160

what would make me happy! She made me enter that beauty contest. I didn't want to win any beauty prize. But I did win it, and what happened? I was rushed out to Hollywood before you came home from college. So I didn't get to see you or anything. Then *she* wrote me all that gossip about you being engaged to Mabel, and I was so miserable I didn't know what to do. And those old friends I was staying with kept rushing me around to parties that bored me to death. And then I met Paul Gordon, and the only reason I ever promised to marry him was to get even with you for taking up with that horrible Mabel!"

"I never did, baby. I swear—"

Shivering with wet and cold, she hugged her coat around her. She was beginning to look like a bedraggled kitten, and the only thing warm about her was her heated, angry voice. "Then I got your letter. And all I could think of was how I could get to see you. I thought I'd just plain die if I didn't. So I arranged for you to get a job in Hollywood. I was taking a chance, but I did it. And then I took another chance, a big one, to fly to St. Louis to see you. And I took another chance, phoning Aunt Clara to ask if she'd help me so you and I could be together for a few days. So what do you do?"

Her next words came in a quiet rage. "You're chicken, Bob Connor. You don't want to take a

161

chance on anything. You keep saying it's because you love me so much. Well, I don't happen to believe you! If you really love a person with all your heart, you don't keep worrying about what's wise or how things will turn out. You just love her, and you want to be with her, and you'll take a chance on anything. You'll even take a chance on it turning out all wrong. If you won't do that, your love doesn't amount to much."

She saw another cab cruising along and gestured to the driver. "I'm going back to meet Aunt Clara," she said over her shoulder as she stepped into the cab. "Good night."

"Okay, honey. You win." He followed her into the cab and closed her in his arms. "I'll go to Aunt Clara's," he said. "But, woman, I am not going to marry you."

"Want to bet?" Susan said sweetly. She smiled her lovely smile, and she put her arms around him and hugged him tight while the cab sped back through the rain.

Chapter Fourteen

The next morning, in Hollywood, there was also a rainstorm, one of those freak California storms. Big round hailstones pounded against the roof and clattered against the window panes. There was wind along with the rain, a fierce wind approaching gale proportions that shook the little cottage and finally awakened Carol, who had fallen into a deep, dreamless sleep just before dawn.

She had lain awake for hours, trying to make up her mind what to do about going back to the office to work. If she went back, she knew that Jerry would take it as a tacit surrender. He would assume she was back to stay, that she had gotten over Saturday's disappointment, that everything between them was exactly as it had been for years.

163

It would be one more assurance that he could treat her as he pleased and get away with it.

That was the way it had always been, and that was the way it would be again—unless she did something about it.

Well, this was the time to do something and make it stick if she was ever going to. She would have to be ready to cope with Jerry, who would argue and cajole and plead, telling her how clever and fine and beautiful she was, how the office couldn't get along without her and neither could he; how she was the only girl he had ever loved. But this time she would know how to handle him. Since her love for him had dissipated into nothing more than a half-sad, half-bitter tenderness, it would be easy.

So the only big problem was the financial one. Fortunately, she had a little money saved, and she could always sell the house at a small profit. By cutting corners and managing with what she had, she could get along until she found another job, or made up her mind if she dared gamble: borrow money from the bank and start a little interior decorating shop of her own.

The decision brought peace to her restless, troubled mind. Having made it, she fell asleep instantly, and when she awoke and heard the storm banging at the house, it was pleasant to lie there, listening to the angry wind outside, and know that she didn't have to get up until she felt like it.

For one day in her life she was going to do exactly as she pleased. She was going to shut the world out. She was not going to worry about anything or anybody.

"And I'm not going to answer you the whole day long!" she said aloud, glaring at the phone as it began to ring.

The phone didn't own her, did it? It wasn't her master, was it? People were always talking these days about communication with other people. Well, a phone was simply a convenient way of communicating with the outside world, and this was a day when she did not want to communicate.

So she let the thing ring.

And ring it did, almost steadily, for the next hour. Carol ignored it, except for two of three exasperated times when she snapped: "Oh, shut up, why don't you?"

It was Jerry calling, she felt certain. When she didn't appear at the office by ten-thirty, Jerry would be in quite a state. To Jerry's way of thinking, she should be as dependable as the United States mail service. Neither rain nor storm nor sleet . . . She showered and dressed and fixed a nice breakfast. She was fairly hungry. I wonder if Susan is back yet, she thought once, and immediately reminded herself to forget Susan. And as for Paul Gordon . . .

Because of the way Jerry has treated me, she told herself, I was becoming a frustrated, disgruntled old maid. And frustrated old maids get jittery over any attractive man who looks at them twice. That explained Paul's attraction for her, explained it perfectly. So that settled that.

She washed her breakfast dishes and straightened up the kitchen. She went to the living room window and stared out at the storm. And all the time, with intervals of a few minutes in between, the phone continued to ring.

Then it stopped ringing . . . and thirty minutes later there was a loud, insistent hammering on her front door. When she opened it, she was confronted by a man she scarcely knew at first, his eyes looked so wild, his face so gray.

"Jerry!" she exclaimed. "Are you ill?"

"Let me come in and sit down," he gasped, and stumbled past her into the living room. She could tell he'd been drinking, perhaps quite a lot. Never before had she known him to touch liquor in the morning. When he did drink, it was strictly for social purposes.

He sat down. "Don't you know what's happened?" he said. "Haven't you seen the morning paper?"

He stared at her. Then he began to shake and

tremble and buried his face in his hands. "Oh, Lord," he moaned, "how am I going to live with myself after this! I feel like a murderer. In a way, I am."

Carol crossed the room and knelt beside him. She took his hands away from his face and made him look at her.

"Jerry, would you please tell me what's wrong?" she said. "No, I haven't seen the morning paper, or had the radio on. What has happened?"

"Susan Starr!"

"Oh, Susan." Then she said the first thing that popped into her mind. "Don't tell me she's eloped with her Bob and isn't coming back. That would be a sweet mess."

"She's dead," Jerry said.

"What?"

"That plane she was coming back on last night —they think the pilot hit a heavy fog and flew too low. The plane crashed into the side of a mountain; there were no survivors. Oh, no, there isn't a chance that Susan wasn't on it; her name was listed among the passengers. Oh, Carol, what am I to do! I feel as if I were directly responsible for her death."

He grabbed her and held on to her in utter desperation. "Help me, Carol. Don't just stare at me. Say something."

"What do you want me to say?" Carol demanded, as soon as she could get free of his clutching hands and rush to the bedroom to get a coat and her bag.

Jerry was right at her heels, unwilling to let her out of his sight or reach, as if she were a life-line, and without her he'd be lost. "I want you to tell me it *isn't* my fault," he said thickly. "Oh, I know it is. I'm responsible for her going. You warned me, but I wouldn't listen. I was wrong and you were right, as you always are. But say you forgive me, Carol. Please, please say you forgive me." And he fastened his arms about her and buried his face against her shoulder while shuddering sobs racked his body.

She had never seen a man cry like that before. It was awful to hear him, to feel his hands clutching at her.

"Who am I to say I forgive you, Jerry? I'm not God."

"Somebody has to," he moaned. "I've done a terrible thing. She was so young, so beautiful, so alive." He raised his face. "How can I go on living with myself, knowing that she'd still be alive if it weren't for me and my bright scheme to make a few dollars?"

"What you really want," Carol said carefully, "is to forgive yourself. Well, I can't do that for you, Jerry. That's up to you. Now you listen to me." Abruptly her voice toughened as she

168

watched him through the mirror where she had gone to smooth back her hair before she tied on a scarf.

His eyes were still blurred with tears, and his mouth was working helplessly. It was clear to Carol that he was suffering from self-pity, plus a guilty conscience. Well, it was no good encouraging that sort of thing. Like everybody else, Jerry had to stand up and face the consequences of what he had done; face it like a man, not weep and wail like a stricken baby.

She turned away from the mirror. "You can't go on like this, Jerry. It's true that you encouraged Susan to take that trip, but you didn't force her to go. And you certainly have no responsibility for the plane crash. It's a ghastly, horrible thing. But it's one of those tragedies that no one could have foreseen, and for you to blame yourself as if you were directly responsible is nonsense. So pull yourself together, honey."

"It's all very well for you to talk." He took hold of her hands again. "You're so strong, so wise. Carol, promise me something. Promise you'll never leave me!" But he wouldn't give her a chance to promise or not to promise. He went on talking. When he had read the awful news in the paper that morning, the first thought that came to him was: Thank goodness I have Carol to go to!

Yes, she thought, as she went back to the mirror to see if the scarf was tightened sufficiently to protect her hair when she went out in the rain: when he was in trouble, she was the one he thought of first. And as she drove her nails into the palms of her hands, she could not be sure if the resentment that tore through her was resentment against him for running to her when trouble came, or resentment against herself because she could not bring herself to desert him at such a time.

I can't turn my back on him when he needs me, she thought, and walked back to him, caught his hand and told him to come along. "We're going to see Susan's mother," she said, pulling the collar of her red coat close around her throat.

For the first time Jerry seemed to be aware that she was dressed to go out. "Are you out of your mind?" he asked, shocked at what she had said. "How could I face that woman? You know I couldn't."

"I know you'll have to," Carol said emphatically.

She reminded him of the fact that Susan's mother knew nothing about where Susan had been, why or how she had gotten there. "No one knows but you and me, Jerry. It's up to us to go and tell her how it all happened. I hate going as much as you do. But it's our responsibility, and we've got to face up to it."

Then she thought of another thing she'd have to

face sooner or later: telling Paul Gordon. She stood for a moment, her face drained white, unaware that Jerry had gone into the bathroom to get a drink of water.

Bitterness, hate, and a measure of contempt would be in his eyes when she told him the whole truth about Susan's ill-starred journey. Oh, he couldn't blame her that Susan had gone. But he could say: "Had you told me the truth, I would have stopped her from going. It was all so unnecessary. I told you I'd be glad to arrange for her to see her boy friend, that I'd have gotten him here myself if I'd known how to go about it. Didn't I tell you that? But instead of taking me at my word and confiding in me, you helped cover up for her and sent her to her death."

Jerry came back into the room, looking slightly more like himself. "Okay, honey. If we've got to go face the music, let's go and get it over with. But you still haven't promised to do what I asked you."

"What was that, Jerry?" She really had forgotten, or almost.

"Never to leave me!" He pulled her close. "I really love you, honey. And one of these days we'll get around to getting married, honestly."

"Will we?" The sadness in her smile was caused by her lack of interest in marrying Jerry. She wondered why it had ever seemed the most important thing in the world to her. "I won't desert you," she said, "as long as you need me."

Chapter Fifteen

When Jerry knocked on the door of the apartment, which was in a four-story building on a side street, three or four blocks from Hollywood Boulevard, there was no answer at first. "Let's go," Jerry said. "This is no time to barge in on the poor woman with a lot of explanations. What good will that do? If she's in, she probably wants to be alone with her grief. Honestly, honey, I don't think we have any right to intrude just now. Come on."

"Sh," said Carol. "I heard someone moving around." She pushed Jerry aside and knocked more vigorously with the brass knocker.

After another short wait, the door opened and Carol's heart dropped about a thousand miles below sea level when she saw Paul Gordon. She wasn't yet ready to face him.

"Hello," he said, and stepped out into the hall, closing the door carefully behind him.

"If you came to see Susan's mother, you'll have to excuse her. Mrs. Starr doesn't care to receive any visitors today. She has a headache."

The casual, offhand way he said it caused Carol to stare at him. Maybe this was what was known as keeping one's feelings under Spartan control. Of course she wouldn't have expected Paul to be the kind to break down, to exhibit his grief like an hysterical woman. Still, the man was human, wasn't he? You'd think his face would at least look a bit haggard, a little strained.

"I hardly know what to say," Carol began. "We've seen the papers; we know about the tragic thing that's happened to Susan. There are times when words are inadequate. I know what a shock this must be for you."

"Yes. I was shocked, all right."

Paul pulled out a cigarette, offered the pack to Jerry who shook his head, then remembered to say: "I'm sorry, Gordon. Not much a man can say to another man at a time like this, but—well, this thing has shaken me up. It really has."

Paul got his cigarette lit. "Well, that's life for you," he said, his voice evincing no emotion whatever. "Hard to know what to expect from one minute to the next."

It was the shock of it, Carol decided. It *had* to be that, because no man—certainly not Paul—could be as cold-blooded as he sounded. Even if he hadn't been altogether sure about marrying Susan, he had loved her enough to *ask* her to marry him, to shower expensive gifts on her, to plan his future around her. So his casual, offhand manner simply made no sense, unless he was so numbed that he hadn't as yet grasped the horrible reality of Susan's death.

"What we really came for," Carol said, "was to explain to Mrs. Starr how Susan happened to be in St. Louis. Jerry and I feel terribly guilty about that part, because—"

"I take the blame for that," Jerry interrupted, his voice grim with self-denunciation. "Actually, it all started more or less as a joke. I jokingly asked Susan how she would like to fly to St. Louis, and she took it seriously. What it was all about—"

"Post-mortems never help much, do they?" Paul cut in curtly. "What's done is done, and we might as well let sleeping dogs lie, as they say."

Well, Carol thought, he doesn't act like a man filled with sorrow, but he certainly is full of clichés. She looked at him thoughtfully, lifting her hands to tighten the scarf around her head. "Don't you think Mrs. Starr would want to hear how her

175

daughter happened to be on that plane? It wouldn't lessen her grief, but it might serve to relieve her mind. She must wonder——"

"Frankly, I don't think it would serve any useful purpose," Paul said. "It might even do considerable harm in a way that I'm not free to explain to you. No." He shook his head most emphatically, and then he amazed Carol, *really* amazed her, by asking her to meet him out at the Honeymoon House that afternoon. "Say around two o'clock," he said, glancing at his watch.

"I want to have another look at the house before I sign a contract," he said.

"You're going to buy that house?" Carol said. "Now?"

Even Jerry looked slightly startled.

"Why not?" Paul inquired pleasantly. "I've intended to buy it. I thought I explained that."

"But that was before—before Susan—" She hesitated, shrinking from the awful finality of the word "died."

"I think it would please Susan if I went through with my original plan, just as if nothing had happened to change anything."

"Very well," Carol said in a curiously flat tone. "I'll meet you at the house." And she managed to hold back what she was thinking until she and Jerry were in his car and on the way to his office.

Then she burst out: "I never in my life saw a

176

man act and talk so queerly. Honestly, Jerry, do you suppose the shock of Susan's death was too much for him, and that it's affected his mind?"

"He's gone batty, you mean?" Jerry thought it over. It could be, he supposed. Meanwhile Jerry's own downcast spirits abruptly took a decided turn for the better.

"If he's serious about buying that house, that's one thing we won't have to cry about."

"Jerry!"

"What's wrong about saying that, honey? You know how this thing has hit me. Believe me, it gave me a real jolt. But life has to go on, and so does business. So why pretend I don't want to get rid of that house?"

"I wouldn't get my hopes up too high," Carol warned him. "I'm beginning to wonder if Paul really knows what he's saying or doing. He may not even show up this afternoon."

"Well, if he does, don't discourage him about this sale."

"Oh, I wouldn't think of doing that," Carol said coldly.

Paul showed up. In fact, he was waiting in his car when Carol drove up in front of the house and as they went up the outside stairs the first thing he mentioned was the weather; how beautifully the sun shone on the glistening wet foliage, now that the storm had passed.

"Yes. It's turned into a very nice day," Carol agreed as she fitted her key into the lock and led the way in.

If it were I, she thought grimly, and I had just died a violent death, and Jerry went around saying what a beautiful sunshiny day it was, I'd come back and haunt him.

The hour that followed was not only strange; it was downright weird.

To start with, Paul informed her that he did not wish to discuss Susan, the accident, or any of the chain of circumstances which led up to Susan being in St. Louis when she was supposedly in Carol's house in Sierra Madre, only a few miles from Hollywood.

"Don't you think you owe it to me to hear my explanation?" Carol asked him. After all, he had said some very unkind things to her over the phone. He had implied that she was a liar; that she was playing some kind of a deep devious game with Jerry Powers. "Just because this tragedy has happened, Paul, it doesn't mean that I was double-crossing you in any way. There's such a thing as not betraying another person's confidence, you know."

Very true, Paul agreed pleasantly, but he still did not wish to discuss Susan's doings except as they concerned this house.

There, of course, Susan's name could not very

178

well be avoided because, after a manner of speaking, he was buying this house for Susan. He wanted it completely furnished and decorated, exactly as if he had been going to bring Susan into it as his bride. Moreover, he wanted the job done quickly, because it was possible that he might be returning to Texas by the end of the week.

"Do you think you could get everything fixed up in three days?" he said. "The furniture selected and moved in, the drapes up, the linens stored in the closets? Oh, and you might get a landscape gardener if you know of a good one."

Naturally he didn't expect to get plants and trees and flowers growing within a matter of days. But it wouldn't hurt to get a garden arrangement worked out and under way. "Might get a few shrubs planted," he suggested, "so the place won't look so bare outside. Nothing like some green stuff to add charm to the appearance of a house."

"Paul, have you lost your mind?"

Now that was a fine thing to say, to say to a man who obviously was still in such a state of shock that his mind refused to accept the awful thing that had happened! That *had* to be the explanation. She was sure of it now. But if you saw clearly that a person was unbalanced, the last thing you should do was mention it. That wasn't even polite.

However, the words had simply popped out before she realized what she was saying.

He smiled gently.

"In other words, you think I'm crazy," he said, "because I've decided to buy this house and fix it up, just as I would have done if Susan and I—"

"I think it's morbid," Carol said. "I've heard of husbands who wouldn't allow anything in a house to be changed after they lost their wives. Even that is a sign of a sick mind. But to buy a brand-new house, and furnish it, and plan a garden, and—"

She walked to where he was standing by the window, looking down to where the garden would be, and when he said thoughtfully: "I think a rose garden would be nice, there to the left," tears welled in her eyes as she touched his arm and said with deep compassion: "Oh, Paul, how you must have loved her! You said that you didn't know for sure how you felt about her, but your heart knew! Paul, I'm so sorry." Impulsively she held her cheek to his, but only for a second.

The next second his hands were on her arms, holding her away from him. His voice was harsh. "Don't be sorry for me, Carol. Sympathy from you is one thing I can't take. I mean that, Carol. Now about the house: can you attend to everything in the next two days?"

"I thought you said three." Even that was impossible. It meant selecting furniture for a seven-room house; deciding on color schemes; finding exactly the right drapery materials, rugs and carpets; not to mention getting the things delivered, arranged, rearranged, all the rest of it. It would take three weeks just to get things started.

"Well, do the best you can in two days," Paul said. "Let's say the living room and one bedroom."

He made quite a point of the bedroom, which he wanted to be worked out around Susan's personality. "I'll leave the color scheme and details to your judgment," he said.

And then he went on for quite a while about his ideas as to a woman's bedroom. It was a place where she spent so much of her time, did so many personal things, such as creaming her face and brushing her hair. "We'll want a lot of mirrors," he said. Mirrors where Susan could have seen herself from every angle, if she had sat there brushing her beautiful hair.

"I told you, I think," he said, his voice strangely gentle, "what gorgeous hair Susan had." And of course Carol had had a chance to see for herself that night. "The moon was bright enough for you to see her hair, wasn't it?"

"Yes." Carol's voice couldn't have been gentler. Poor guy, she thought pityingly. He really has gone over the borderline. Mirrors! "The moon was bright and I could see her hair. It was very lovely, just as you said it was."

"Well, do you think you can do the two rooms in two days?"

"I'll try."

"Very well. I have to be out of town tomorrow, so I'll leave it all up to you. I'll meet you here Thursday afternoon. And, Carol?"

"Yes, Paul?"

"Don't waste time or energy feeling sorry for me. Don't feel badly about Susan, either." He hesitated. "Susan went on this trip because she wanted to be with her old sweetheart, you know."

Carol looked at him. "Yes, Paul, I know. But I didn't realize that you knew."

"Oh, yes, I know. Bob Connor. His name was on that passenger list, you know. Her mother recognized it immediately."

"That must have given Mrs. Starr a turn," Carol couldn't resist saying with a bitter smile.

"Yes. It upset her considerably. Well, as I started to say, Susan did exactly what she wanted to do. If she had a chance to start over, regardless of how things might turn out, I suspect she would do the same thing."

"Are you saying she would have preferred dying with her Bob to going on living without him?"

He gave her a slow, strange smile. "That's one

way of putting it, yes." And then he said that he had to hurry back to Susan's mother, who shouldn't be left alone.

He went off in quite a rush, leaving Carol in the house to wander from room to room, to study the bedroom which was to be fitted up so that a girl who was lying dead at the foot of a mountain would have plenty of mirrors in which to look at herself as she sat brushing her gorgeous mahogany red hair.

Presently she sat down on the floor and wept; wept for the beautiful young girl whose life had been snuffed out, and for the man who had cracked up because the loss of two sweethearts by violent death had been more than he could take.

Everyone had a breaking point, and Paul had reached his. She wept because she felt so sorry for him, felt such compassion. But she also wept because she could have loved him so greatly, and he didn't love her at all. He had only thought that he did, for a very little while.

Chapter Sixteen

Afterwards, Carol would always wonder how she got through those next two days without losing her own mind; or at least dropping dead from exhaustion, frayed nerves, short temper, and the nervous stomach she invariably developed when she had to argue and act mean, if necessary, to pressure other people into doing things they said were utterly impossible.

"Are you kidding?" Obviously the pleasant young carpet salesman with the wavy blond hair and nice smile really did think it a joke. Have the carpet for two rooms delivered and laid that same afternoon? "Here at Parker Brothers, Miss Kane, we are very proud of our prompt, friendly service. But if you read our ads carefully, you'll notice that we do not undertake to perform miracles."

"But you do want this order, don't you?" Behind the sweetness in her voice, the charm in her smile, was a veiled threat.

This would be a large order before the house she was doing was finished. And there were other stores, many others, that would be only too delighted to perform a few miracles when it meant that at least two thousand dollars would change hands.

"Shall we say that the men will be there at one o'clock, then? Thank you *so* much; you've been *very* obliging!" And with a cordial smile Carol was on her way to select chairs and divans and a bed and mirrors and a dressing table and a few cushions and pictures and ornaments so that the house would begin to look like a real home; not just an impersonal hotel apartment.

And finally, of course, she had to select the right drapery material which had to be made up and hung, practically with the speed of light.

And with each and every purchase, large or small, she had to fight the same stubborn resistance against her unreasonable demand that delivery plus any necessary service be made within the next few hours.

They were right, of course. It was unreasonable to expect salespeople, store managers, delivery men and skilled workers to knock themselves out catering to the demands of a girl who sounded a bit irrational.

They had no way of knowing, of course, that she, like an idiot, was knocking herself out trying to meet the deadline set by a man who was more or less a mental case.

The more Carol thought about it, the more she considered Paul's strange talk and the absolute ghoulishness of this house business, the more convinced she was that Paul really was temporarily deranged.

She had no time to go to the office, but she phoned two or three times. Jerry seemed to have recovered nicely from his feeling of remorse and guilt. He seemed his old self again, with a few new irons in the fire, a few new worries about some deals that hadn't come off.

"Don't kill yourself over this job for Paul Gordon," he advised Carol. But on the other hand: "Don't forget we'll be sending him a good stiff bill. We need it and he can afford it."

That sounded pretty cold-blooded, considering the circumstances. But maybe Jerry's attitude was the right one. After all, had Paul considered her physical endurance or her nervous system when he had asked her to do this utterly impossible job?

But impossible things can somehow be done occasionally, and when Thursday afternoon arrived,

Carol was ready. Rather, the two rooms were more or less ready.

She herself was ready to collapse. Such trivial matters as lipstick and a hairdo were things of the past. She had on a yellow sweater, blue denim pants and sandals. She looked awful. But she was still breathing, and the rooms were ready, and when Paul came she took him straight into the bedroom, which she considered a work of art.

"I had to rush like mad," she said, "but I'm really proud of this room. I hope you like it, too."

He stood there looking it over.

Carol had done the room in a deep, lush forest green as the basic color. The carpet, the spread on the over-sized bed, the drapes closing over the sliding glass doors that led out into a side patio, all were that deep, restful green. It was like walking into a cool, dim forest. Except for the mound of scatter cushions on the bed, the only contrast was made by the two white ivory love goddesses on the small tables on either side of the bed. And wherever you looked, there were mirrors reflecting the white goddesses of which Carol was inordinately proud. She had discovered them in an Oriental store, and she hadn't needed the aging Chinese proprietor's assurance that they were extremely rare pieces.

"It's all wrong," Paul said when he finally spoke.

187

"I beg your pardon?" She simply couldn't believe what she was hearing.

"All wrong," he repeated.

"Wrong!" Carol exclaimed, a steely glint in her eye. "How can you say that, Paul? It's a beautiful room."

"Yes," he agreed pleasantly, "it is beautiful. But it would never do for Susan. It's too sophisticated." He turned to look at her. "I'm afraid you've created a room to please yourself, Carol; not an eighteen-year-old girl-bride."

Carol stared at him. Her teeth bit down hard on her underlip. And then, very suddenly, she knew that she couldn't take any more of it. She was too tired, her nerves were too shot. She had tried so hard, and this was the thanks she got.

Well, all right then. She was through taking it, through holding back what she was thinking.

She flung words at him like so many bullets. "You're crazy as a loon. That's the kindest thing I can say about you, Paul Gordon. If I didn't do this room to please myself, whom would I please? That poor kid who will never walk into any room again? Girl-bride! Is your mind so warped and twisted that you really believe Susan will be anybody's bride? Or are you simply trying to see how hateful you can be? Maybe this is some crazy idea of yours to punish me. Maybe that's it. Is it?"

"Punish you?" He watched her for a good thirty

seconds before he said: "Why should I be trying to punish you, Carol? For what?"

"Oh, you know for what." She was breathing hard. "Because I didn't tell you that Susan was flying to St. Louis."

"Oh, that."

"Yes, that! And even if it isn't that—" her voice was shrill and furious— "no matter what it is, even if you *are* crazy, this is the worse piece of ingratitude I've ever seen. I tried so hard to get this room done on time, to make it lovely to please you. I wore myself out. I'm sick, really sick, I'm so tired. And now—now—"

Because she had really reached the end of her rope, she ran to the bed and threw herself down on the beautiful new forest-green spread, and the tears came. The wild, hot, salt tears streamed down her cheeks as she turned to look up at Paul, who was leaning over her.

"Please don't cry, Carol."

"I can't help it. I always cry when I'm angry and tired. Oh, Paul, how can you act, talk the way you do about a girl who can never come back to you?"

"Well, you're right in a way, Carol. Susan isn't coming back to me but she'll be back. She'll be right in this room, and that's why—"

"Paul! How can you? Susan is dead. Don't you realize—"

He smiled gently, touching the tears on her cheek with his fingertip. "No, dear. Susan isn't dead. She wasn't on that plane, fortunately. She changed her plans at the last minute."

And then he told her. Susan had phoned him on the morning of the plane accident. She hadn't wanted him or her mother to be worried. She had told Paul the whole truth about everything. She had also told him that she wanted to be released from her promise to marry him. Bob was the only man she could ever be happy with, and they were going to be married at her aunt's house before they returned to California. "They're due back tomorrow morning," he said. That was why he had wanted something done about the house as quickly as possible.

"I love Susan as if she were my sister," he said. So he had wanted to do something really nice for her. And what could be nicer than to give her and Bob the house for a wedding gift?

Carol sat up, and hot, raging anger gathered inside her. "Why didn't you tell me?"

"I couldn't, Carol. I promised Susan—"

"Jerry was half distracted because he felt responsible for having let her go. Why didn't you tell him there was nothing to feel guilty about?"

"I gave Susan my solemn promise, Carol. I was to tell her mother that she was safe, but nothing more. If her mother had known that she and Bob

190

were getting married, Mrs. Starr would have moved heaven and earth to stop it. Don't you see how it was?"

Carol was up off the bed and streaking into the front room where she had left her bag and cardigan. "I see nothing except that you let me make a fool of myself. I sympathized with you, pitied you, worried about you. I thought you'd lost your mind from grief! And all the time you *knew*."

"I had given my word to Susan," he said, "to tell no one."

"You could have told me in confidence. I don't betray a confidence. You knew I wouldn't. But instead you worked on my sympathies, got me to tear myself to pieces working on this house, all because I felt so sorry for you."

She was at the door, had opened it. Then she turned to glare at him for the last time, and her mouth fell open as she heard what he was saying in the gentlest of voices.

"Are you very sure you did it all for me, Carol? Are you very, very sure you weren't considering Jerry's interests? I'm fairly sure he'll send me a nice fat bill for your services."

"Is that what you really think of me, Paul?"

His expression was a curious mixture of doubt, sadness and hope. "I love you," he said softly. "I'm sure of that much."

They were the last words she had expected to

hear, and for a moment her heart lifted—but only for a moment. For how could she believe it?

"Love!" she said bitterly. "You have a strange way of showing it." And she slammed the door and was gone.

Chapter Seventeen

Carol drove straight home, drank some warm milk, swallowed two aspirin tablets, undressed and got into bed. She fell asleep almost instantly. It was the sleep of utter exhaustion, and she was lost to the world until ten o'clock the next morning when the phone awakened her.

"I am not coming to the office today," she said when she heard Jerry's voice, "or any other day," she added. "So there's no use asking me how soon I can get there."

Her head was still groggy from so much sleep; she still felt more dead than alive. But she could recall dimly that on her way home the day before she had decided that what she needed was a nice long vacation. She needed to get away from the unreasonable demands of selfish men who worked on her sympathies and good nature to get her to do the most preposterous favors for them.

Apparently, she had reasoned grimly, men take one look at me and spot me for an easy mark.

Jerry had done it for years, with his promises to marry her. And as for Paul Gordon; it had taken him only a matter of days. Just go ahead and kill yourself from overwork, if necessary. Only get the job on the house finished. All in good time, I'll explain that Susan is perfectly safe, that she's a very much alive, blushing bride. And what if I did take a slight advantage of your sympathetic nature? You shouldn't worry so much about other people's troubles if you don't want them to use you to further their own ends.

Apparently Jerry was in one of his more belligerent moods. "What do you mean, you aren't coming to the office today? You've got to come! And the sooner you get here the better. Paul Gordon is here and—"

"I have nothing to say to Paul Gordon," Carol said icily. "If I never see the man again I can live happily. You might tell him for me—"

"Now see here, Carol. You seem to have gotten out of bed on the wrong side. You seem to forget that there's a business deal involved. Gordon is here to sign the contract for that house."

"How nice for you, Jerry dear."

"But he refuses to sign unless you're here as a witness."

"Oh?" She couldn't have been more laconic. "Well, that isn't so nice. For you, I mean. Because I'm not going to be there."

"And there's another matter he wants to talk over, but he insists that you be a party to the discussion."

"Indeed? Well, you tell Paul Gordon for me that I am not interested in anything he has to discuss. If he wants Susan's house worked on some more before she arrives, let him do it himself."

"That's wonderful news about Susan, isn't it?"

"Yes," Carol said. She cradled the receiver and got up to shower, dress and fix her breakfast. She had had her orange juice, one piece of toast, and two cups of coffee when she heard a car drive up outside.

"Since Mohammed wouldn't come to the mountain—" Paul began when she opened the door. He was grinning.

Jerry, right behind him, was also smiling, but it was a forced, painful smile. Needless to say, Jerry didn't approve of leaving his office at ten o'clock in the morning, and wasting a couple of hours driving back and forth to attend to a matter that could have been finished within ten minutes.

"Let's not have any stalling around," Jerry said when they were seated in the living room. "I have a thousand things to attend to today. I have a luncheon appointment that's very important. Have you a pen, Carol? I seem to have left mine on my desk."

Carol produced a pen, and Jerry got the contract of sale for the Honeymoon House from his briefcase. Then Paul changed chairs, settled himself comfortably, lit a cigarette, and announced that he had just about decided to advance the money for the acreage around the house. Also, he would put up whatever money was necessary for Jerry to get started with his project of a villa on the land.

It wasn't, Paul explained, that he was interested in making more money. His problem was what to do with the money he had. He intended to endow a hospital, and any extra that came along could go into that.

While Paul was talking, Carol sat watching Jerry, who sat with an unlit cigarette between his lips, watching Paul a little as if he were hypnotized. There was a strange gleam in his eyes and his lips twitched nervously. He's excited by the prospect of making some really big money, she thought. If this went through, it could mean that Jerry would be a rich man: the thing he's dreamed about his whole life long! That was why he looks practically bewitched. She felt a strange, sudden pity for him. She felt sorry for anybody to whom money was a kind of god; a false god that could be so easily snatched away!

Jerry leaned forward, jerking nervously at his collar. His eyes never left the other man's face. "Are you serious about this, Gordon? Because if you are—" He turned his shining eyes toward Carol. "Do you realize what this could mean, honey?"

"Of course," she said quietly. She sat very still. She, too, was watching Paul. Somehow she sensed that there was a catch in his generous offer.

"What's the catch in all this, Gordon?" Jerry asked abruptly. His smile was vaguely worried. "I mean, this is a pretty big thing you're offering to do. What am I supposed to do in return?"

"Do for me, you mean?" Smiling cheerfully, Paul uncrossed his legs, then recrossed them. "Not a thing. There is one condition, however. Carol here has put herself out considerably for me. I'd like to do something nice for her in return. Well, I happen to know how close you two are to each other. I understand how much your success means to her. I know how she's worked along with you, put so much of herself into your business.

"I also happen to know that you two have been planning to get married, but something always

197

came up to interfere at the last minute. Well, as the saying goes, there's nothing like killing several birds with one stone. So my plan concerning this property is to sign all the necessary contracts and give them to Carol as a wedding present. Naturally, it will be necessary for the marriage to take place first.

"Well, there you have it, Powers. Not much of a catch to that arrangement, is there?"

"I should say not!" With the pleased, delighted laugh of a man who had just hit the jackpot, Jerry was out of his chair, had his arms around Carol and was pulling her to her feet.

"Did you hear that, honey? Did you hear what the man said?" He was all beaming excitement. "All we have to do is get married, and I've made it. So what are we waiting for? Grab a lipstick and an extra sweater, and we'll start for Yuma." He was trying to kiss her, was much too elated to notice that she avoided his lips.

"You mean start now?"

"Sure. Why not? We can be there by evening, get the marrying business over with first thing in the morning and be back here by late afternoon. How about having dinner with us tomorrow evening, Gordon? We'll have a little celebration dinner and sign the papers. That okay with you?"

She felt ashamed for him, absolutely sick with

198

shame, and disgusted with herself when she thought of all the years she had wasted loving him.

She moved a little away from Jerry before she spoke. Somehow she managed to keep the venom out of her voice, the bitter tears out of her eyes. "I want you to leave this house," she said. "And don't ever come back. I never want to see you again as long as I live. Is that clear?"

She added tightly: "In case it isn't clear, Jerry, I'll spell it out for you. I am not part of a package deal, like the cheap tin spoon in a cereal package that nobody ever wants."

She said a lot more. In fact, getting angrier as she went along, she expressed all the bitter recriminations she had kept to herself for years, through one heartache and disappointment after another. She said all she had to say, and it felt good to get it out of her system.

At first Jerry didn't believe a word she uttered. He simply stood there watching her, amazed by her unprecedented outburst, but not believing she really meant any of it. Everything would be okay as soon as she cooled off and calmed down. That was what his expression said. After all, she loved him, didn't she? She had, for these many years. It stood to reason she couldn't have changed overnight.

Then it hit him! She did mean it! That was when he caught her shoulders, and his handsome face turned ugly with anger and frustration and something close to hate. "Do you mean to tell me you'd ruin this deal for me? Don't you realize what this means to me, Carol?"

"Sure," she said, pushing him away. "It means your chance to get into the big money. It's a pity you have to pass it up. But you couldn't get around to marrying me when there was nothing in it for you; you waited until there was nothing in it for me. Now I haven't the faintest desire to marry you, Jerry. Surely you wouldn't expect me to go off to Yuma, put myself to a lot of inconvenience, go through a ceremony with a man I no longer love, just to be sweet and accommodating, would you?"

Jerry left finally, looking beaten and furious at the world in general.

"Well, what are you waiting for?" But she didn't sound angry, only very weary, as she turned to Paul, who showed no intention of leaving for years to come. "You've had your fun. You made me see Jerry for exactly what he is: a man whose heart works like a cash register. You made me see how I feel about Jerry, too. If I had any further doubts, you cleared them up for me. I suppose I should thank you for that. But do you think it was kind to humiliate me?"

She went to the divan and buried her face in her

hands. "I feel so ashamed! He jumped at the chance to marry me—if he could make a lot of money on the deal."

Paul went to the divan and sat beside her. "I didn't intend to humiliate you, Carol. I simply believed the time had come for you to face up to a few stark facts about Jerry, then make up your mind what you wanted to do."

"I had already faced those facts, Paul. I didn't need to have them jammed down my throat until I choked on them."

He put his arm around her lightly, comfortingly. "No," he said. "Your confidence in your love for Jerry was slipping but you still had some feeling for him. You were still vulnerable where he was concerned. By the way, if it's any comfort to your pride, I believe he does love you—as much as he is capable of loving any girl."

"Yes, perhaps. But that isn't very much, is it?"

"There are men who are incapable of loving deeply, Carol. It isn't their fault; it isn't the fault of the girls who are unlucky enough to fall in love with them. Jerry is one of those men, and I wanted you to see it for yourself. It's no reflection on you that he cannot give you the kind of devotion that isn't in him to give."

"No, I suppose not." She turned her face, giving him a sad little smile. "Our love lives don't seem to go very well, do they?"

"Mine is going very nicely, thank you, as far as it has gone." He laughed softly, as if over some secret joke. "If you were referring to Susan, I assure you I couldn't be happier about the way things have turned out. I always wanted a sister, and that's the way I love Susan: like a dear, sweet, beautiful sister. I want to indulge and do nice things for her. By the way, she got in this morning. I met the plane, and I met her Bob. He's very much okay, to my mind; a nice, clean-cut, serious-minded boy who will make Susan a good husband. I've decided to give him a job, to let him try his hand at looking after my affairs out here. That will be a break for him and Susan, and it leaves me free to get back to Texas. How would you like to go back with me, Carol?"

She didn't know if he was serious at first.

"Of course," he went on, "I haven't an awful lot to offer you, honey. I expect to give most of my uncle's money away. I meant what I said about endowing a hospital, so you wouldn't be marrying a rich man."

"Did I ever say I wanted a rich man?" she interrupted.

"No." Then he was silent for a moment, as if busy dragging something from his memory. "As I recall, you said that first day on the phone—"

"Don't mention that phone business, please."

"But it's important." He was smiling as his arm drew her closer. "You were very definite about what you wanted: to build a home that would be filled with love, for a man who would think you were the most important thing in the world to come home to. Well, I'm that man, sweetheart."

He swung her around, holding her so that her face was directly under his. "Right now," he said thickly, "there are only two things in this world which matter to me. One is that I love you. After long years of weary waiting, I've come on a beautiful, warm, loving woman who can fill my life completely. I had such a girl once and I lost her. Now I've found you. It's like being given a second chance at paradise."

She saw the passionate tenderness in his eyes, and her whole being seemed to melt with the wonder of the miracle that was happening to her. "What is the other thing that matters?" she asked softly.

"Do you love me, darling? Because nothing would be any good if you don't. It has to be a two-way business, you know. And I want to know that the girl I'm going home with to that Texas ranch house thinks that *I'm* the most important thing in the world. I want it all, sweetheart; all the love there is in your heart to give. Can you give it to me?"

There weren't any words to answer a question like that. So Carol didn't bother with words. She simply put her arms around his neck, and when his lips closed over hers she co-operated in creating the kind of a kiss that would be a precious memory for both of them forever.

After a long time—maybe an hour or so—Paul let her go long enough to remind her: "By the way, honey, about this ranch house—I'd better warn you, it's no Hollywood Honeymoon House. There are no electronically controlled gadgets, no doors swinging open and shut without the touch of a human hand, no sun rising up out of the ceiling. It's just a plain little old house with a big open fireplace, heavy wooden beams, and a few mice scampering around in the walls. How does that sound to you?"

"Like the most perfect Honeymoon House of all time," Carol told him with a radiant glow in her eyes that said she meant every word of it. "How soon do we start?"

Paul considered.

Well, first they had to be married. How about Yuma for that? Yuma seemed to be the place where there was no waiting or red tape. What about tomorrow, Saturday? Would that be soon enough? He was grinning at her.

Tomorrow was perfect! Carol agreed. After all, Saturday was her favorite day for marriage, Yuma

204

her favorite place. So why change, simply because this time she was really going to be married?

This time it was going to be the right time, the right place and the right man.